Ice

Linda Howard is the award-winning author of many *New York Times* bestsellers. She lives in Alabama with her husband and golden retriever.

Also by Linda Howard

ICE

A NOVEL

LINDA

HOWARD

piatkus

PIATKUS

First published in the US in 2009 by Ballantine Books,
an imprint of The Random House Publishing Group,
a division of Random House, Inc., New York
First published in 2009 by Piatkus

A CIP catalogue record for this book
is available from the British Library

ISBN 978-0-349-40011-2 (HB edition)
ISBN 978-0-349-40012-9 (TPB edition)

Printed and bound in Great Britain by
MPG Books, Bodmin, Cornwall

Papers used by Piatkus are natural, renewable and
recyclable products sourced from well-managed forests and certified
in accordance with the rules of the Forest Stewardship Council.

Mixed Sources
Product group from well-managed
forests and other controlled sources
www.fsc.org Cert no. SGS-COC-004081
© 1996 Forest Stewardship Council
FSC

Piatkus
An imprint of
Little, Brown Book Group
100 Victoria Embankment
London EC4Y 0DY

An Hachette UK Company
www.hachette.co.uk

www.piatkus.co.uk

Ice

Chapter One

The place never changed.

Gabriel McQueen actually liked that about his hometown, Wilson Creek, Maine. He liked the continuity of it, the security, the solidarity. He liked that his seven-year-old son, Sam, was seeing the town almost exactly as Gabriel himself had seen it growing up. He liked that Sam was building some of the same memories he had.

He liked the little town as it looked during the march of seasons: the budding of spring, the green of summer, the rioting colors of autumn when the twin white steeples pierced a deep blue sky, but his favorite time of the year was right now. The last few weeks leading up to Christmas were special, when excitement and anticipation seemed to grip everyone and the little kids were almost giddy from it all. He could barely wait to see Sam enjoying the same things he'd enjoyed at that age.

He drove his black four-wheel-drive Ford F-250 through the town square, smiling as he saw that every storefront was decorated with tinsel and twinkling multicolored lights, that the big fir tree in front of the courthouse was festooned with so many lights that it looked like a solid blaze that even the cold, steady, miserable mist of rain dripping from the ugly leaden sky couldn't dim.

There was an empty parking space at the end of the metered row in front of the courthouse, and he squeezed the big pickup between the white lines. Jamming his weatherproof cap on his head, he got out and fed enough change into the old-fashioned meter to buy him two hours. He wouldn't be there that long, but he erred on the side of caution because it would be embarrassing as hell for the sheriff's son to get a parking ticket in front of the courthouse on his first day home—not to him, but to his father. Not embarrassing his father was well worth a couple of quarters.

The mist of rain blew in his face; the last weather report he'd checked predicted snow later on tonight when the temperature dropped. Ducking his head against the wind, he quick-timed up the courthouse steps, opened the double glass doors, then took the stairs on the right down to the basement. The sheriff's department still occupied the basement of the courthouse even though the jail was on the top floor and the arrangement was damned inconvenient, but that was how things had always been and Gabriel figured they would still be that way when he died.

The sheriff's department was the first door on the left. The door opened into an area filled with four desks, three women, and a lot of attitude. Behind them was another door, and stenciled on it was *Harlan McQueen, Sheriff.* The stencil had been done almost thirty years before, and in some places the lettering was almost gone, but Gabriel knew his dad was thinking of retiring—had been for the past five or ten years—so, as a thrifty Mainer, he didn't see any sense in having the doors relettered.

All three women looked up when Gabriel entered, their faces immediately wreathing in smiles. All three jumped up with disconcertingly girlish squeals, considering the youngest was a good fifteen years older than he was, and rushed at him; you'd think he hadn't seen any of them in a year, instead of just two months. Somehow he managed to almost get his arms around them all; he was a big guy, but three women were a lot for any man, especially when one of the women was pleasantly hefty.

Two of the women wore brown sheriff's department uniforms; Judith Fournier and Evelyn Thomas were sisters, and their resemblance was strong enough that when they were in uniform and their hair was pulled back and secured per regulations, they were almost indistinguishable. Patsy Hutt, the queen of the outer office, was soft and round and crowned with snow-white hair. Today she wore thick-soled boots, jeans, and a wool sweater decorated with sequined snowflakes. She looked like the most benign woman in the world, but Gabriel had a very clear memory of her swatting his ass when he was about seven and full of self-importance because his dad was the sheriff.

Among the three women, they controlled the outer office and access to the sheriff, ran most of the department, and knew everything there was to know about everyone in the county.

"It's about time you got here," Patsy scolded. "I was getting worried, with you driving in and meeting this storm head-on."

"Storm?" He went on alert, adrenaline surging. "I checked the weather forecast before I headed out; the rain was supposed to turn to snow tonight, but that was all." That had been this morning, at a motel in Pennsylvania. Before leaving North Carolina he'd put snow tires on his truck because, hell, December in Maine meant snow. That was a no-brainer. Since leaving, though, he'd been listening to XM, so he wasn't up to the minute on the weather forecast.

Patsy's concern meant something, however. Mainers were accustomed to winter weather and knew how to handle it, so any looming storm severe enough to get their attention told him a lot about the potential for danger.

Before she could answer, the door behind them

opened and all four looked around. "Gabe," said his father, a wealth of affection and something close to relief in his lined face, and Gabriel tore himself from the clutches of the outer-office tyrants to stride across the floor. He exchanged a brief bear hug with his dad, they clapped each other on the back, then Harlan said, "I'm glad you made it. The weather is turning nasty in a hurry and I need help."

Gabriel's level of alertness ratcheted upward several more degrees. If Harlan McQueen was admitting he needed help, then something serious was going on.

"You got it," he said as they moved on into Harlan's office, which tended more toward cramped than spacious. The county hadn't splurged on the department's offices, that was for damn certain. "What's up?"

His father's sharp gaze showed appreciation for Gabriel's unhesitating support and willingness to act. When he'd been younger, that natural inclination toward action—any action—had sometimes landed his ass in hot water, but as a sergeant in the military police, he'd been able to channel that aggression and decisiveness into the job, which was good for both him and the army.

"This damn weather system is dipping our way," Harlan said tersely. "We were supposed to get snow, with the ice staying northeast, but now the weather service is saying we're going to get hammered by the ice. They issued the storm warning just a little over an hour ago, and we're scrambling to get ready, plus there's an accident tying up three deputies when I can't spare even one."

Shit, an ice storm. Gabriel was on full alert now, his eyes narrowing, his stance subtly shifting as if he could take on the storm in a bare-knuckle brawl. Ice was ten times worse than a blizzard, in terms of damage. Maine had taken two hits from ice in the past ten or twelve years, but both times the storm had missed this area. That was good then, but bad now, because it meant there was a lot of weakened timber that had been spared before but would now be coming down under the weight of the ice, crushing cars and houses, taking down power lines and leaving hundreds of square miles in the cold and dark. Ice was like a crystal hurricane, destroying everything it touched.

"What can I do?"

"Drive out to the old Helton place and check on Lolly. I haven't been able to get her on her cell phone, and she may not know this weather system has shifted our way."

Lolly Helton? Gabriel almost groaned aloud. Of all the people—

"What's she doing here?" he asked, trying to disguise his sudden hostility, which was the way Lolly Helton had always affected him. "I thought the whole family had moved away."

"They did, but they kept the house for summer vacations. Now they're thinking about selling it, and Lolly's here to check things out and, hell, what difference does it make? She's out there by herself, with no way of calling for help if she gets hurt."

Despite his reluctance to put himself out for Lolly Helton, Gabriel immediately grasped the logistics of what his father was saying. Anyone who wasn't from Maine might not be able to read between the lines, but he could. Cell service was spotty at best; if she'd been safely here in town, Harlan would have been able to reach her on her cell phone, but out by the Helton place a cell phone was useless for anything except throwing. And because no one lived in the old house now, the land-line phone service had long ago been disconnected. Probably there wouldn't be any televisions in the place either, for the same reason. Unless Lolly happened to drive into town and was listening to her car radio, she'd be unaware of looming disaster.

Fuck. There was no way out of it. He had to go after her.

"I'll take care of it," he said, striding to the door. "How much time do I have?"

"I don't know. That's a higher elevation, the icing will start sooner than it does here. The weather service is saying it could begin here as soon as sundown."

Gabriel glanced at his watch. Three p.m. This far north, sunset was around four p.m., which didn't give him much time. "Shit," he said. "I won't have time to see Sam."

"You will if you hurry. The kids were let out of school as soon as the weather service changed the forecast, so your mom has already picked him up. I'll call her to get some coffee and food ready for you, stop by there on the way, then haul ass."

He was out the door, moving fast, before Harlan had stopped talking. The coffee and food were more of a necessity than a comfort. He'd been driving all day, he was tired, and in severe weather conditions having something to eat and drink could make the difference between living and dying. He didn't know what kind of situation he'd be in, once he left the main road and started the long, winding climb toward the Helton place, so it was better to have the provisions and not need them than it was to not have them and maybe die because of it.

The wind slapped him in the face as soon as he opened the courthouse door and stepped out. That wasn't good. The air had been fairly calm when he went inside, but now, barely ten or fifteen minutes later, it was really blowing. Wind made the tree limbs and power lines come down faster, besides sapping the body heat of every poor fool who was outside, or who was being sent to rescue some bad-tempered bitch with a snotty attitude who was as likely to tell him to go to hell as she was to park her dainty ass in his truck.

Nevertheless, an unholy grin split his face as he sprinted for his truck, unlocking it with the remote while he was still about ten feet away. He wrenched the door open and vaulted inside. Lolly Helton!

Damn, nobody else had ever locked horns with him the way Lolly had, or got on his wrong side so easily. He probably owed his success in the army to the early training she had given him; after all, how much trouble could the most fractious recruit be compared to Miss Hoity-Toity Helton?

Lollipop! Want me to lick you, Lollipop?

Putting the gear in reverse, he powered out of the parking space in an arc that left him facing the direction he wanted. His grin grew wider as he shifted into drive and put his boot down on the accelerator. The memory echoed in his head, the taunt that he'd known would drive her over the edge, the laughter of his buddies, the way her tight, unfriendly expression had gotten even tighter as she stared at him as if he were an insect she'd stepped on and smashed flat.

That was the thing about Lolly Helton. Even as a little girl, she'd been so convinced that she was so much better than everyone else in town that nothing he or anyone else had said to her had put a dent in that superiority. Her father was the mayor, and she never forgot it, or let anyone else forget it. If she'd been especially pretty, or especially smart, or anything else out of the ordinary maybe she'd have been more popular in school, but there hadn't been anything special about her. He remembered her frizzy brown hair, and that nothing she wore had ever looked very good on her, and that was it. Well, except for the way her expression had said *Eat shit and die, peasant.*

There had to be something wrong with him to actually feel a sort of anticipation at seeing her—and probably arguing with her—again.

Keeping a steady hand on the wheel, he switched the radio from XM to a local station so he could catch any weather updates. Within a few minutes he left the city limits of Wilson Creek behind, speeding up to gain whatever extra seconds he could. Another kind of anticipation built inside him, sharp and strong. Sam. He was going to see his kid again in just a few minutes, and his heart began pounding with joy.

Four miles down the road he turned between two huge spruce trees onto a concrete driveway. Behind the spruce trees was a sprawling white house with neat black shutters and a three-car detached garage. The back door was already slamming open as he lurched to a stop, a small, dark-haired dynamo erupting from the house yelling, "Dad! *Dad!*"

Gabriel left the truck running and leapt out, barely in time because Sam launched himself upward. He grabbed the kid out of midair, and skinny arms wrapped around his neck so tightly he could barely breathe. He didn't need to breathe. He just needed to hold his son.

"We got out of school early!" Sam said, beaming at him. "There's going to be an ice storm. Gran's making plenty of soup, because she said we'd probably need it."

"That's good to hear," Gabriel said. Sam was wearing a coat but it wasn't zipped, and the hood had fallen back so the cold rain was falling on his bare head. Gabriel pulled the hood up, then opened the truck's back door to grab his duffel, shouldering the door shut. Holding his son in one arm and the duffel with the other, he ran through the rain to the back porch. His mother was standing there, trim and capable-looking in her jeans and boots, the wide smile on her face not quite disguising the concern in her green eyes.

"He wouldn't wait," she said, throwing her arms around Gabriel and hugging him, then planting a swift kiss on Sam's cheek as well.

"Ah, Gran," he said, squirming, but he didn't wipe his cheek. Gabriel grinned, remembering how mortifying it had been at that age for his mother to kiss him. Sam might as well get used to it, because nothing stopped Valerie McQueen from kissing the people she loved.

He dropped his duffel, set Sam on his feet, then squatted and began rifling through the duffel for his knife and flashlight. "The coffee's almost ready," his mom said. "I already have one thermos filled with soup, and here's one of your father's insulated rain ponchos." She gave him the poncho, then turned and hurried back into the kitchen.

"Thanks," he said, hoping he wouldn't need it. His boots were all-weather and insulated, so his feet should stay warm and dry, but he tucked an extra pair of socks in his coat pocket, just in case. His coat was thick and heavy and he had gloves in the truck, as well as a blanket that Sam had shoved under the backseat over a year ago and which he'd never gotten around to dragging out. He figured he was as ready for a quick trip up the mountain as he was going to get.

"Where are you going?" Sam asked as he watched the preparations. "You just got here." Disappointment laced his tone, edging into sulky.

"I have to rescue a woman from her house on a mountain," Gabriel replied, keeping his own tone brisk so Sam would know this wasn't the time for an argument, but he put his arm around him for a quick, hard hug. "I don't want to leave either, but when something needs doing, someone has to step up and do it."

Sam mulled that over. With Gabriel being career army and his grandfather a sheriff, in his short life he'd heard a lot about responsibility, and seen it in action. He might not like it, but he understood it. "Is she hurt?"

"I don't think so, but your grandpa wants me to get her before the ice storm leaves her stranded."

Sam gave a solemn nod. "Okay," he finally said. "If you have to. But be careful."

"I will," Gabriel promised, wanting to grin but keeping his expression grave. His little guy was learning how to step up to the plate himself.

Valerie returned, and he stood to take the two big thermos bottles from her. "Be careful," she said needlessly, echoing Sam, but now that he was a parent himself he understood that the worry never stopped, no matter how old or how capable he was.

"Aren't I always?" he asked, knowing that would make her roll her eyes, which it did. He kissed her cheek, then knelt to give Sam another, extra-big hug. "I'll be back as soon as I can. Can you take care of Gran until then?"

Sam nodded solemnly, and he squared his thin shoulders. "I'll do my best," he replied, though the look he gave his grandmother said that he doubted he could control her. Gabriel bit the inside of his cheek to hold back a grin.

"Bring Lolly here," Valerie said briskly. "Don't try to take her into town and then make it back. We have plenty of room and plenty of food, so there's no point in pushing your luck with this weather."

"Yes, ma'am," he said obediently, but inside he was thinking: *Oh, shit, I'll be stranded with Lolly Helton.*

Maybe she wouldn't be there. Maybe she was somewhere safe in town, and had simply turned off her cell phone. Maybe he'd slide off the road and have to walk back, and wouldn't be able to make it up the mountain to the Helton place. Maybe, even if she was there, she'd refuse to go anywhere with him. Yeah, he could see that.

Then that weird sense of anticipation rose in him again, the antsy feeling he got when he knew he was going to be in a fight and was actually looking forward to it. He'd been in a lot worse situations than this, he thought. He'd waded into brawls with nothing but his fists, kicking ass and breaking heads, and come out of it okay. Lolly had a tongue like a scorpion, but that was about it. He could handle her and anything she dished out. "Thanks," he said to his mother. "I'll see you in about an hour." Then he dashed back out into the cold rain and the deepening gloom, off to fetch the spoiled princess from her mountain.

Chapter Two

Earlier that afternoon

The old white Blazer, crusted with grime and salt, turned into the small parking lot of the local grocery store. A skinny, ill-kempt man with straggly, dirty-blond hair pulled the Blazer so it was facing the road and put the gear in park. "Ready," he said, drumming his fingers rapidly on the steering wheel. "I'm ready. Ready to go." The words were fast and abrupt. "You got the gun?"

"Right here," the woman beside him said, shoving a pistol into her stained, red canvas tote bag. She was as skinny and straggly as he was, her eyes and cheeks sunken, her long, dark hair plastered to her head so that her ears stuck out through the strands. Her gaze roved restlessly around the parking lot, darted to the front of the grocery store, back to the parking lot. She put her hand on the door handle and shoved the door open, then quickly closed it again when another vehicle turned into the parking lot and drove past. She watched as a black Mercedes SUV, driven by a lone woman, went past them with tires hissing on the wet pavement and parked in a slot close to the store door.

"What're you waiting for?" the man asked, still drumming his fingers. He shifted restlessly in the seat. His name was Darwin Girard, and he hadn't slept in three or four days, maybe even longer. Despite that, he felt as if he might explode with energy, and just sitting there was almost more than he could handle.

"That woman looked at me." Niki Vann indicated the driver of the black Mercedes as the woman got out of the small SUV and pointed a remote at it. The lights blinked, signaling that the vehicle was locked, and the woman hurried through the rain into the little grocery store.

"She did?" Darwin asked, his attention zeroing in on the woman like a laser. No one was supposed to notice them. That was the plan, and he didn't like people messing with his plans. Feral hostility glowed in his sunken eyes as he glared at the door through which she'd passed.

"Yeah. Bitch," Niki growled, for no reason other than that the other woman was driving a Mercedes. Then an idea began to squirm in her brain. "I bet she's got a lot of money in her purse. Look at what she's driving. I bet she's got more than that rinky-dink little grocery, and she's by herself."

Darwin drummed his fingers faster, faster. "What're you thinking?" he asked, as if he didn't know, grinning at her. Niki was even better than he was at seeing an opportunity and not hesitating to act on it. Because of her, their supply of meth was fairly steady. She was always looking for a way to get more money.

She shoved the Blazer door open again, and got out. "Be back in a minute," she said before closing the door, then she darted through the rain, her thin body almost dwarfed by the huge green jacket she wore.

Inside the store, Lolly Helton grabbed a cart and headed down the first aisle. She didn't need much, just some cans of soup and a couple of sandwich items, maybe a couple of magazines to read, and she wanted to be home before dark so she was in a hurry. Because she was in a hurry, of course, she was stopped almost immediately.

"Lolly!" said a woman wearing a bright red apron that covered her from neck to knees, looking around from where she was neatening the stacks of produce that had been disordered by customers picking through them for a perfect head of cabbage, or apples that were either firm or soft according to their individual tastes. "I heard you were back. You're looking well."

"Thank you," said Lolly, good manners making her pause. "You, too. How have you been?" Mr. and Mrs.

Richard had owned the little grocery store for as long as she could remember, and she'd always liked Mrs. Richard, who loved to joke and gossip and never had anything negative to say about anyone. The door opened behind her and a gust of cold air swept in. She didn't look around, but moved her cart to the side so the newcomer could pass by.

"Well. Busy, this time of year, with all the holiday cooking." She wiped her hands on the apron, her gaze moving beyond Lolly to whoever had entered the store behind her. She gave a brief nod of acknowledgment, then turned her attention back to Lolly. "Where are you staying tonight?"

"At home," said Lolly, a little startled. Where else would she be?

"Goodness, child, haven't you been listening to the radio? They're predicting ice for tonight."

An ice storm! As if she could see the approaching storm, Lolly turned and looked out the window, her gaze sliding past the woman who had entered behind her. It wasn't anyone she knew—didn't look like anyone she'd *want* to know—so she didn't make eye contact. "I haven't had the radio on," she admitted. She seldom listened to the radio anyway, preferring her own CD collection for music.

"You can't stay way out there by yourself. If you don't have anyone you could stay with, Joseph and I have an extra bedroom—two of them, in fact, now that the boys are married and gone."

Lolly's mind raced. She didn't have any old school

friends she could stay with for the duration of the storm, mainly because she hadn't really been friends with anyone. Her school years hadn't been good ones. She was much better at making friends now, but that meant all of them were back in Portland. She didn't like the idea of staying with Mr. and Mrs. Richard— she liked them, but she wasn't close to them—but with an ice storm looming she had to make some fast decisions.

"Thank you, I'll take you up on that offer, at least for tonight," she said, lifting her purse from the cart. She wouldn't need any groceries, after all. "I need to go home and get some of my things. How much time do I have?"

"The weather service said it should start around dark. Don't tarry."

Lolly checked the time. She had a few hours, but the icing could start sooner than that at home because the house was at a higher elevation. "I'll be back as soon as I can," she said. "I can't tell you how much I appreciate the offer."

Mrs. Richard made a shooing motion with her hand. "Go on, hurry!"

Lolly did, though she took the time to return the cart to the small corral, pushing it past the woman wearing an oversized green jacket and carrying a dirty red canvas tote, as if that was her nod to the Christmas season. A sense of urgency drove her to almost run back to her vehicle; an ice storm was nothing to dismiss. Snow was nothing, at least to a native Mainer, but ice was unbelievably destructive. She could have been stranded for days, even weeks, if she hadn't happened to stop by the grocery store and talked to Mrs. Richard.

So much for her plans, she thought ruefully as she wheeled out of the parking lot, but a looming ice storm trumped packing. There weren't even that many personal items left to pack up, so it wasn't as if she had to get everything done right now. The house had been used so seldom in the past several years, there was just the bare minimum of furniture and some odds and ends left, anyway. She had intended to take her time packing—in fact, her actual plans for the night had been to heat some soup, turn on the gas fireplace, and read, leaving packing for tomorrow morning. She enjoyed the peace and quiet, and there was something about being snug in a warm house on a snowy night that deeply appealed to her.

She had come here this week wanting to enjoy a few leisurely days in the house where she'd grown up, wallowing in warm fuzzy memories and, in her own way, saying good-bye to the house and to Wilson Creek. With her parents in Florida and her job keeping her busy in Portland, there was no need for a vacation home that was so rarely used.

The Helton house had once been the finest in the county, a large and somewhat extravagant—for the area—two-story house on the mountainside, just outside of town. For a lot of years all the important local political meetings and parties had been held there, which Lolly found slightly ironic, as she was the only family member left in Maine and she had no interest in politics and even less in partying. She'd outgrown some of her youthful awkward shyness, but she'd never be outgoing. She much preferred an evening at home to a night on the town.

She didn't look forward to staying with the Richards, preferring to be on her own, but she'd deal. She worked for an insurance company and had learned, out of necessity, how to interact with people. As a child and, even worse, a teenager, she'd always hung back, never knowing exactly what to say and certain no one wanted to talk to her anyway. She'd hidden all those painful insecurities behind a wall of hostility, so it wasn't surprising she hadn't had any real friends here. She didn't know why she kept coming back, but she managed at least one trip almost every year. She wished she could afford to live here, in the house where she'd grown up, but Wilson Creek simply didn't have much in the way of job opportunities, and she didn't have the money to open her own small business.

The windshield wipers swished back and forth, clearing away the light rain that hadn't varied in intensity all day. There was something unnerving about the sheer unchanging relentlessness of the rain, as if the very lightness of it was proof that Mother Nature didn't need to make a dramatic statement to squash civilization like a bug. All it took was a rain not much heavier than a mist, and some cold air in the right po-

sition, to wreak havoc. She felt a chill run up her spine; even though it was hours yet until nightfall, the gloom was deepening, and she had to turn on her headlights. She hadn't met any traffic since turning on this road, and that in itself was kind of spooky. For a moment she felt the urge to turn around, buy some pajamas and underwear in town, and dart for the safety of the Richards' house.

Then she saw the blur of a vehicle behind her, too far for her to make out any details, but just knowing she wasn't alone on the road was enough to settle her nerves. She'd allow herself fifteen minutes, no more, to gather what she needed and head back to town. She should be safe and secure well ahead of the storm's arrival.

Within minutes she had turned off the main road and was carefully navigating the narrower road that wound up the side of the mountain toward the house. She still knew every curve, every tree and rock, of this road, because she had driven it so often after she'd gotten her driver's license. Even before that, her mother had taken her to school every day, and picked her up in the afternoons, so for almost her entire life she'd had at least two trips a day up and down this mountain. The road held no surprises for her, no fears; it was the weather that made her anxious.

Her sure-footed SUV, bought used three years ago because she'd needed a dependable four-wheel-drive vehicle, climbed steadily. Visibility dropped as the mist grew heavier. She took a quick glance at the outside temperature gauge and saw that the temp was just a couple of degrees above freezing. The trees had a faint silvery cast to them; was ice already beginning to form?

Then she turned into the driveway, powering up the long slope toward home. It wouldn't be "home" much longer, she thought, but right now it still looked welcoming and somehow just right. Never mind that the house was almost sixty years old, had faded a bit, and sagged here and there; it was still large and solid, offering a warm, safe refuge on a wintry night. Too bad she couldn't stay here, but if she got iced in it would be a couple of weeks before she could get off the mountain, depending on how bad the damage was and how many trees came down.

Much as she loved this place, she knew it was time for the house she'd grown up in to be home to a family again, as it had been home to her. Once the few remaining personal effects here were packed away, sold, or stored, her childhood home would go on the market, and it would no longer be hers in any way. Too bad she wouldn't have the few days of escaping into the past that she'd wanted, but the weather had other plans.

She didn't bother with parking in the detached garage, just pulled up close to the front porch. Keys in hand, she hurried up the steps and unlocked the front door. As soon as she let herself in she shed her heavy, hooded winter coat, tossing it over the newel post and dropping her purse on the bottom step.

Detouring to the back, she grabbed her snow boots from the mud room and brought them to join her coat and purse.

She didn't know when she'd be able to come back, she thought as she started up the stairs. Was there anything in the refrigerator she needed to clean out? No, she didn't think so. She'd been eating granola bars for breakfast, not bothering even with milk for cereal, and at night she'd either had peanut butter and jelly sandwiches or picked up a sandwich in town. She knew how to turn off the water at the valve, and turn off the gas to the water heater; other than locking the door, that was all she could do to get the house ready to withstand the coming storm.

She was halfway up the stairs when she heard the rumble of a vehicle. She stopped, then reversed her path. Knowing the people here as she did, she wouldn't be at all surprised if someone had heard about the storm, realized she was here with no television or phone, and come to collect her. This had always been the kind of community where neighbors looked after neighbors, and she missed that—some days. She was both glad for the company and concerned at the delay.

Crossing her fingers that she wouldn't have any trouble getting down the hill, Lolly opened the front door. She expected to find someone she knew, an old friend of her parents or the closest thing she had to a neighbor, and a welcoming smile was on her face. The smile froze when she realized she didn't know the rough-looking couple coming up the porch steps, though the woman looked vaguely familiar. Then Lolly remembered seeing her in the grocery store earlier, recognized her even though the stringy dark hair was now partially covered by a knit cap, and a thick coat disguised her thinness.

A couple of possibilities rapidly crossed her mind. Were they lost? Looking for shelter? Maybe they were unfamiliar with the area and didn't know that they did *not* want to be stuck here on the mountain if the ice was as bad as predicted.

"I'm just on my way out . . ." Lolly began.

The man right behind the stringy-haired woman pulled a gun from his parka pocket. Shock hit Lolly like a slap in the face; she gaped at the gun, barely comprehending what she saw, then she sucked in a quick breath and instinctively stepped back. The man and woman both rushed at her, shoving her back inside so roughly that she slammed hard into the newel post, staggered, saved herself from falling with a desperate grab at the wood.

The man shoved the door shut behind them. The woman glanced around, at the living room on the left, the flight of stairs straight ahead, the dining room on the right. She smiled, showing discolored and rotten teeth. "See, baby, I told you she was alone."

Lolly clung to the newel post, literally frozen under the sudden lash of terror, her brain numb, coherent thoughts scattered before they could even form. She groped for understanding, and finally, like a switch being flipped, her sluggish brain began to function. Home invasion—*here*, in Wilson Creek! It was so wrong, that something like this could happen here, that sheer indignation abruptly shoved terror aside and suddenly she could move, was already moving even before she realized. She ran, ran for her life.

The man shouted, "You bitch! *Fuck!*" as Lolly darted through the dining room, dodging around the table, grabbing one of the heavy chairs and slinging it in his path then racing into the kitchen. Footsteps thudded behind her but she didn't look, didn't spare even a split second, just ran for her life. If she could just get outside—

She grabbed for the doorknob, and a hand grabbed her hair. Pain laced her scalp; her head jerked back and she was sent spinning away from the door. Her feet went out from under her and she fell to the floor, the man's grip cruelly tight on her hair. He shoved her down and she hit the cold, hard linoleum face-first.

Lolly screamed, then caught her breath and held it. She grabbed for her hair, trying to pry his hands away. The sudden weight of his body on hers was heavy and hot. He pressed her into the floor, forcing her breath out, and she couldn't take another.

"Now you got me all excited," he whispered in her ear, grinding himself against her bottom. His breath was hot and fetid, and a rough stubble scratched her cheek. She turned her head away from the stink and roughness, but she couldn't move far. Her fingers scrabbled at the linoleum, trying to find purchase, trying to find something, anything—

There was nothing. A kitchen was full of weapons, but none of them were on the floor.

He began tugging at her jeans, trying to pull them down.

Damn it, *no!* Both panicked and enraged, she instinctively fought back, slinging her elbows back as far as they would go, trying to hit him. She wiggled and bucked and squirmed, trying to throw him off, but he was too heavy and she was in a helpless position, flat on her stomach on the floor.

He couldn't get her jeans down. He shoved his hand under her and fumbled with the button and zipper, grunting like an animal. Lolly pressed her hips harder to the floor, trying to mash his hand so he couldn't get the zipper down, but he jerked her head up and slammed it down on the floor again and white spots swam in her vision. Dazed with pain, she went limp for a second and he shoved his rough hand inside her jeans, against her bare belly.

She was going to die. He was going to rape her, and kill her. Her last minutes alive would be filled with unspeakable terror.

Tears filled her eyes, and she screamed. The sound was rough and raw, like an animal's, the noise tearing from her throat. She didn't want to die; she didn't want her last memory made in this house to be a nightmare. She screamed again and again, unable to stop herself.

He shifted upward, lifting his weight from her. She gulped in a deep breath and tried to gather her strength, then he rolled her over and started yanking again at her jeans.

"Don't," she said, sobbing. "Please. Please don't." She hated to beg but she couldn't seem to stop herself, and what did pride matter anyway? She'd do anything to get him to stop. Desperately she searched for some reason she could give him, something that would appeal to him. "I can pay you. I can give you all the money I have."

He didn't seem to hear her at all.

The kitchen was dim, with only the scant light from the window, but she could see that he was almost as thin as the woman, most of his teeth were dark with rot, and his eyes . . . they were strangely wide open and feral, glittering with something that was inhuman.

Drugs. He had to be on drugs, both of them did. There wouldn't be any reasoning with him, so she stopped trying. He continued jerking at her clothes and she kicked, she screamed, she clawed at any patch of skin on him she could reach, but his coat was heavy and protected him from her nails, so she went for his face. He couldn't hold both her hands and undress her at the same time, so she punched and clawed at him with every ounce of strength she had, but the blows didn't seem to affect him at all.

He got her jeans halfway down and reared back to

unzip his own pants. Laughing, he clamped one hand around her throat and leaned his weight on it. She couldn't breathe, couldn't reach him . . . her vision grayed, and she couldn't see anything except his grinning face above hers. *Tunnel vision,* she thought vaguely, and knew she was about to pass out. If she did, she'd be entirely helpless, and his maniacal face with the rotten teeth would be the last thing she ever saw.

Desperate, on the verge of unconsciousness, she tried to jerk her knee up. He shifted, blocking the movement, and laughed.

"Darwin, you son of a bitch!" the woman yelled in a grating tone.

The overhead light came on, the lights shining right in Lolly's eyes and blinding her. The weight on her throat eased and she coughed, sucking in air. Darwin was very still. "I was just having a little fun," he said sulkily.

The woman with the stringy hair stood over them both, and with blurred vision Lolly looked up at her. There was no sympathy in the woman's face, no woman-to-woman empathy, nothing but fury. She had a gun, too, and she had it pointed at Darwin's head. "Get up."

"Now, Niki," he began, belatedly placating as he realized where the pistol was pointing. "Baby, I—"

"Don't 'baby' me, you two-timing son of a bitch."

Darwin's gaze shifted from Niki, back to Lolly. She

saw the animal in his eyes, saw him weighing his options. He smiled a little, and then he forced Lolly's thighs farther apart.

Niki swung her pistol and hit Darwin on the side of the head with it. He yelped, and finally . . . *finally* . . . moved off of Lolly. "Fuck, Niki, you could've killed me!" he shouted, getting to his feet and pulling up his pants from where they'd drooped over his skinny ass. "Are you fucking crazy?" He grabbed a dish towel and pressed it to the bleeding wound on the side of his head, where the pistol had split the skin.

Lolly struggled to pull her jeans up, scooting across the floor as she did, toward the back door and icy freedom. Maybe these two bags of shit would kill each other. She was dimly shocked by the violence of her own thoughts, but if she could just get away, she didn't care what happened to them.

Niki's gaze swiveled from Darwin to Lolly, and so did the pistol barrel. "Where the hell do you think you're going?" she spat, then glanced at something in her hand. Lolly froze, blinking. "Lorelei Helton. Portland," Niki said, and Lolly realized the something was her own driver's license. Niki had apparently been going through Lolly's purse while Darwin had been trying to rape her. "What the hell kind of name is 'Lorelei'? It sounds like a hooker."

Lolly didn't bother arguing, just nodded her head in agreement.

"Get up," Niki said, and Lolly obeyed, using the motion to take another step back, toward the door.

Could she beat both of them, and a bullet? They were druggies, they were likely high right now . . . their eyes were wide, the pupils shrunk down to tiny dots. How clearly could they think?

Clearly enough. Darwin suddenly said, "Whoa there, bitch," and lunged across the kitchen to place himself between her and the back door. He shoved her forward.

Niki shook her head and stuck the driver's license in the front pocket of her baggy jeans. "For a woman driving a Mercedes, you don't have much money on you," she growled. "Where's the rest?"

Lolly tried to think, to reason. Her heart was pounding, she was shaking from head to toe and nausea roiled her stomach, but she could still think. Right now, her brain was the only weapon she had. "In the bank. We can go to town and I'll give it all to you, I swear I will, just . . . don't kill me." She shot a glance toward Darwin. "And don't let him near me." If she could actually get to town with these druggies, she'd find a way to escape . . . to get help.

"They'd be closed now, right?" Niki asked, looking at the last gleam of light that pressed against the windows.

Dear God, she couldn't spend the night in the house with these two. Her stomach lurched, and she barely controlled the urge to vomit. "Yes, but I know the bank manager," she lied. She had no idea who the manager was now, and she had never banked here anyway. The first and only account she'd ever opened was in Portland. Would they realize that, if she lived in Portland, she wasn't likely to have an account here? Desperately she plunged ahead. "He'll open up for me. We can leave right now."

Niki considered it, her head tilted to the side and her feral, too-wide gaze locked on Lolly, but after a couple of seconds she shook her head. "No, he'd get suspicious if you did that. We'll wait until morning."

Lolly's heart lurched, just like her stomach. She felt the hard beats hammering inside her chest. The ice was coming; by morning there would be no way down the hill. The road would be a sheet of ice, and she'd be stuck here with these two. She heard what sounded like frozen rain hitting the kitchen windows; maybe it was already too late.

Niki gestured with the gun, waving Lolly forward. Lolly followed the silent direction, passing the woman with the gun more closely than she liked, exiting the kitchen and walking through the dining room with Niki directly behind. When they reached the living room, Lolly saw the contents of her purse scattered across the couch and floor. Her key ring, with the key to the Mercedes between the key to this house and the one to her apartment door, was resting between two cushions. If she could get to the Mercedes, she'd take her chances driving on ice. Even if she slid off the side of the mountain, that was better than being stranded with these two. She needed those keys . . .

Niki gave Lolly a shove toward the staircase. "Go on," she said, jabbing the pistol barrel hard into

Lolly's spine. Lolly took the stairs, her knees shaking so badly she half-expected to fall at any moment. Niki led her to the bedroom closest to the head of the stairs, which happened to be Lolly's own room. "Any guns in the house?" Niki asked brusquely as she switched on the lights and looked around the neat, sparsely furnished room. "And don't lie, because if you say no and we find some, I'll shoot you in the face. Got it?"

"No, no guns," Lolly said, her voice shaking so much her words were barely understandable.

Niki opened all the drawers, gave the contents of the closet a cursory glance, and was satisfied. There wasn't much here, so searching wasn't exactly a chore. There was Lolly's underwear in the top drawer of the chest, some pajamas, and four clean changes of clothing hanging in the closet. Niki looked out the dark window, noting the two-story distance between the window and the ground with some satisfaction. Lolly looked, too, but at the window. Was that a film of ice already forming on the glass?

Niki's crossed the room, and Lolly stepped out of her way. "I'll be watching this door from downstairs," she snarled. "If it opens even a crack, I'm going to send Darwin up here to deal with you." She glanced at the simple lock on the doorknob, and smiled. "And don't think that flimsy lock will do you any good, not when we have these *keys*." She indicated the pistol in her hand and took imaginary aim at the lock, making a shooting noise, then she grinned.

The sight of those rotten teeth made Lolly shudder, but suddenly something she'd heard, or read, clicked in her brain, and she realized what drug these two were likely on:

It was meth—another type of ice, and just as deadly.

Chapter Three

Dazed, Lolly listened to Niki's footsteps as the woman descended the stairs. Voices drifted up from the living room, angry at first, and then softer. Darwin laughed. The sound sent a shudder rolling through her body, which seemed to be the signal that now her brain could allow her body to feel again because she suddenly felt like one huge, head-to-toe ache.

She began trembling. Her shoulder and side hurt from being shoved into the newel post, her scalp ached from her hair being pulled so viciously, and her cheek and one side of her head throbbed from being slammed into the linoleum. Her heart was pounding so hard she thought she might yet be sick, and she felt both sweaty and icy cold at the same time.

Shock, she thought, just before her knees wobbled

and she collapsed on the side of the bed. That didn't help much; her vision tilted, as if the world was turning over, and she toppled to the side. She lay there panting, trying to control her breathing, but the raw, ragged sound of her gasps filled the quiet room.

Knowing what was wrong didn't make her feel any better. If Darwin had come through the door right then, she'd have been completely helpless.

Dear God. What should she do? What *could* she do?

She didn't know what she could do, but one thing she did know: she'd rather die than let Darwin touch her again.

The thought propelled her to a sitting position, and though her head swam she forced herself to stay erect. There was a very strong probability she was going to die anyway, but she'd be damned if she'd huddle there, sniveling, waiting for them to do whatever they wanted with her. She'd rather freeze to death in the ice storm than just sit here like a helpless idiot.

One thing she wouldn't do was make things easy for them. Moving as cautiously as she could, both because she was still dizzy and because she didn't want them to hear her moving around, she eased over to the door and turned the lock. Niki was right: the lock was too insubstantial to stop them for long, but at least she'd have a moment of warning before they walked in on her.

With any luck she wouldn't be here when they decided to return, because she'd rather take her chances with the ice than with them. She took a deep breath, willing her head to stop spinning, and went to the window to look out. Yes, there was definitely ice on the window, and very little light left as the pressing clouds brought a premature twilight. She didn't have much time, because conditions were only going to get worse.

The ground below looked so far away that her instincts screamed she'd kill herself if she jumped, but she didn't intend to *jump*. It was a straight drop from her window to the ground below, with no roofline or eave to assist her, but there were sheets and a couple of thin blankets on the bed. The down comforter was probably too thick and bulky to be useful, but if she tied the bottom sheet to the top sheet to the blanket and then tied the makeshift rope off well, she'd be able to get close enough to the ground to drop down safely.

Swiftly she ripped all the covers from the bed and began tying her makeshift rope. The sheets were easiest, because they were the thinnest. She knotted the first corner to the foot of the bed, tugging hard to make certain the knot would hold; she'd never been a Girl Scout, wasn't a sailor, didn't know a damn thing about knots beyond tying her shoes. She just hoped a regular old knot would be sufficient.

After the sheets came the two thin wool blankets. She would love to have one of the blankets to huddle in as she made her escape, but she needed both of them for length, since the best place to tie off the rope was the end of the bed and it was eight, maybe ten feet from the window. She had always loved the spaciousness of the house, but now that space was working against her. She couldn't move the bed, not without attracting more attention than she wanted. She had to get out, and she had to do it quietly.

When that task was finished, she forced herself to sit quietly for a minute, to give her racing heart time to slow. She was sweating a little, and that wasn't good. One of the first rules of surviving in the cold was not to overexert yourself, because that caused sweating, which would freeze on the body and cause hypothermia to set in even faster.

Then she shook her head at herself. Hell, it was raining; she was going to get wet, anyway. How was a little sweat going to make things worse? She must still be a little shocky, addled but functioning. She just needed to function a little faster, because at any time they might come up those stairs to check on her.

She took every piece of clothing available out of the closet and the chest of drawers, tossing them onto the bed. Before she went out the window, she needed to get as many clothes on her body as possible. Her big, heavy, weatherproof coat and boots were downstairs, so her only chance of surviving the cold rain and ice was to keep dry as long as possible, and that meant layers . . . a lot of them.

Quickly she kicked off her shoes, then stripped off her jeans and sweatshirt and began pulling on thin layers. She'd brought a pair of insulated long underwear and she put that on first, then began pulling on

T-shirts, the thinnest first, the looser ones on top. One flannel shirt, the one she wore while lazing about, she laid aside to tie over her head. There was one pair of old sweats, as well as the sweatshirt she'd been wearing, but before putting on the bulky stuff she stopped to tug on as many pairs of socks as she could fit on her feet.

Her shoes weren't waterproof; her feet *would* get wet, no way around it. The only question was whether she'd be able to get down the mountain before hypothermia killed her. If she managed that, then she'd worry about losing her feet to frostbite.

Then an idea occurred to her, and as quietly as possible she hauled her suitcase out of the closet. She had brought a jar of Vaseline, which she used to remove mascara. She hadn't bothered with any makeup since she'd been here, so she hadn't even gotten the Vaseline out of the suitcase. Thank goodness she hadn't, or it would now be in the bathroom down the hall with her other toiletries.

Vaseline was waterproof, wasn't it? It was at least water *resistant,* and might be just the edge she needed. It wouldn't keep out the cold, but every little bit helped.

She pulled off her socks and coated her feet with the Vaseline, especially her toes, then put her socks back on, and another pair on top of that. Two pairs of socks was all she could manage and still get her feet in her shoes, so that would have to do.

Next came her jeans, then a pair of old sweatpants. Once her pants were on, she coated the outside of the socks with Vaseline, put on her shoes, then smeared the remainder of the stuff on the leather. That was as waterproof as she could make her feet; maybe, just maybe, the multiple layers would do the trick. After pulling on the two sweatshirts, she felt like the Michelin Man, but she was as ready as she could get.

Lolly tiptoed to the door, pressing her ear to the wood, holding her breath as she listened. The intruders seemed to be right at the foot of the stairs, but from years of living in this house she knew that sounds from both the living room on one side and the dining room on the other carried right up the stairs, because when she was young she'd often listened to the parties downstairs.

The argument over Darwin's attack hadn't lasted long. The voices were lower now, and the occasional bout of laughter sent chills down her spine. She didn't think for one minute she'd survive until morning. Right now Niki planned to take her to the bank tomorrow morning for a big withdrawal, but that plan wasn't going to last. One of them would come to their senses and realize it wasn't going to work, or they'd realize they were iced in. One of them would get carried away, and Lolly would end up dead long before morning.

The voices and laughter stopped. She strained her ears and after a moment she caught some grunting and the occasional moan. Her stomach heaved, but thank God they were otherwise occupied. Now would be the best time to make her escape.

She took one quick look around the room, to see if there was anything else she could use. Only the pillowcases were left, but any covering was better than none, so she stripped them from the pillows and tied them over her head. Her pajama shirt doubled as a muffler. Over that she tied the remaining flannel shirt, and she was as ready as she could get.

Grasping her makeshift rope, once more she tugged on the knot securing it to the bed. Walking backward to the window, she tested the other knots as well. They seemed solid enough; they would have to do.

It was now or never. She unlocked the window and pulled upward on the handle. Nothing happened. She pulled again, putting more muscle into it. Still nothing. The bottom dropped out of her stomach. The stupid damn window was stuck, and if she couldn't somehow get it open, then she was stuck, too. Desperately she gripped the handle with both hands, bending her knees and putting her leg muscles into the effort too, and with what sounded like a deafening noise the window rose a scant inch before stopping again.

She leaned her head against the cold glass, only vaguely noticing how good the chill felt against her forehead. She could do this. She *had* to do this. If necessary, she'd break the glass and take her chances that the noise would be heard. One way or another, she was getting out of this house.

Something thunked against the side of the house,

just below the window, and she almost jumped out of her skin. She didn't know what had made the sound, but what if Niki and Darwin had heard it, and came to investigate? She turned her head to stare in frozen agony at the door, trying to hear if they were coming up the stairs, but this far from the door she couldn't hear anything. Frantic, almost sobbing, she grabbed the window handle and began tugging viciously.

A man's head suddenly appeared on the other side of the window. A squeal almost popped out and she choked, slapping a hand over her mouth. She stared, so frightened she could barely move, and abruptly she recognized him. Her heart leapt, and her knees almost buckled. The relief that washed through her was as warm as the sun she longed for at this moment.

Gabriel McQueen.

Chapter Four

By the time Gabriel reached the turn off the main road, the combination of rain and low clouds had deepened to the point that he needed his headlights on to see. The wind had picked up, too, tossing the trees and whistling around the truck. Wind was bad; it would make the limbs and trees begin coming down just that much sooner.

He would much rather have been with Sam, but he never once thought of turning around and simply telling his dad that he hadn't been able to make it up the mountain. Giving up wasn't in his DNA; he'd fetch Lolly off the mountain if he had to drag her down by the hair, which probably wasn't what his father had had in mind when he sent Gabriel on this mission, but then the sheriff didn't know Lolly the way Gabriel knew Lolly.

She'd always been a spoiled brat, nose in the air, convinced she was better than anyone else. Some kids took teasing well; Lolly wasn't one of them. Hostility had rolled off her in waves. Once she'd looked at him with complete disdain and said, "Worm!" He'd hidden his reaction, but inside he'd been furious that she'd dismissed him so completely with that one word. He was the sheriff's son, he was popular and athletic and invited everywhere, and she thought he was a *worm?* Who the hell did she think she was? Oh, right, she was a *Helton,* and she didn't associate with people like him.

She had held herself separate from everyone else, not part of a crowd, never at any of the parties. Looking back, Gabriel wondered now if she'd ever been invited to any of the parties. Probably—but only because she was the mayor's daughter. None of the kids had liked her, and wouldn't have willingly invited her anywhere. He didn't know if that had bothered her, because she certainly hadn't been a joiner. The only school activity she'd been involved in was keeping her nose buried in a book, if that counted.

He wondered if she was still that way—different, and alone. From the distance of years, he could now also wonder which had come first: her attitude, or the teasing. His own parents seemed to like her well enough. Would his dad have bothered to send him on this errand if it had been anyone other than Lolly

Helton who was out of cell range and possibly unaware of what was coming? Harlan McQueen had been lifelong friends with the Heltons, and that hadn't changed just because the Heltons had moved to Florida, trading ice storms and snow for the occasional hurricane.

Meeting up with her again after all these years should be interesting. He just hoped she wouldn't give him any grief about coming back to town with him.

A new weather bulletin came on the radio, and he turned up the volume to listen; evidently it looked as if the storm was going to take a turn for the worst, and faster than expected. He slowed down, looking at the trees, checking for icing. Surely even Lolly would see the wisdom of getting off this mountain before she got stuck here for possibly weeks, without electricity. Unless she had laid in a lot of provisions, she'd be out of food, too. If enough ice coated the trees some of them would come down, blocking the road. Clearing this road wouldn't be a high priority for the county, because the Helton house was the only one on it. Once there had been a couple of other houses, but one of them had burned years ago, and the other had been so neglected the county had condemned it and had it torn down.

One way or another, he didn't want to waste even an extra minute of time on this assignment. He was going to do as he'd been told, then get his ass off the mountain while he could. He missed Sam every day, but at the base he could bury himself in work. Now, with the kid so close, being away from him was an almost physical pain.

The road took a sharp curve, and curled upward in a steep grade. His tires skidded on the pavement and he took his foot off the gas pedal, letting the truck slow to a crawl. Was the road icy already, or had he skidded simply because of the steepness of the wet pavement? His snow tires weren't worth a damn on ice; nothing was, except chains, but even here in Maine not many people had chains. If the weather was that bad, the smart thing to do was park your ass and wait it out, not go out for a Sunday drive.

Damn her, why couldn't she stay in a house that was more accessible? This damn road wasn't much wider than his truck, and trees overhung the pavement in a way that made him wary as he eyed them. Not only would they be deadly if the ice got bad, but they made the road even darker by blocking out whatever light was left.

The temperature gauge on his truck said the outside temp was thirty-two degrees now. Great. Just fucking great. Even as he watched, the digital readout changed to thirty-one. As the road climbed higher, the temp was dropping like a rock. That was ice on the road, all right. He slowed down even more, letting the weight of the truck provide what traction it could.

Turning around wasn't even an option; his truck was too big, the road was too narrow, and the left side was nothing but a steep drop-off. The first place where he'd be able to turn around was at Lolly's house. He was as stuck as a rat on a treadmill, with no way to get off.

His frustration and temper ratcheted up a few notches. If he got up there and no one was home, if Lolly had left town that afternoon and the sheriff just hadn't realized it, Gabriel was going to be royally pissed. He couldn't be mad at his dad, but Lolly was another matter. He might even make a point of hunting her down to tell her what a thoughtless bitch she was.

Odds were he'd find her right where she was supposed to be, though, as cool and detached as always, surprised that he'd show up at her door in the middle of a fucking ice storm when he could be sitting at home with his kid. Hell, he was risking his life to get to her, and that made him even angrier, because he had to stay alive for Sam; his little boy had already lost his mother, and that had been a lot for a four-year-old to get through. Thank God they'd had each other when Mariane died; he couldn't imagine how he'd have made it without Sam. What would Sam do if something happened to him, now? Gabriel couldn't make his mind go there.

The truck powered slowly up the hilly road, but he could feel the tires spinning some, feel the truck sliding to the right as the surface became slicker. The higher he got, the worse it was going to be.

That thought had just formed when he eased into a right-hand curve and suddenly the truck began sliding to the right. This wasn't just the tires skidding; the entire truck moved sideways, the banking in the road, as slight as it was, taking him toward the inside of the curve. As soon as his right tires left the asphalt and hit the shoulder they grabbed traction and began slewing him around, throwing him toward the outside edge where there was nothing but a long drop.

Gabriel shoved the gear into neutral, stopping the tires from grabbing, and let the truck slide back toward the inside. He had no traction, so braking wasn't an option; instead he worked with the truck's momentum and steered away from the edge, toward the mountain side. With a thump, the right front tire crossed the shallow ditch that ran along the inside of the road and his bumper dug into the soft dirt of the bank, bringing him to a stop.

Swearing a blue streak, he stared through the icy windshield at the road ahead.

No way was his truck going to make it up that hill, and no way was he even going to try it. The rain was still falling, a wickedly gentle rain that wasn't heavy enough to run off, which would at least reduce the amount of ice that could form on the trees. No, this was the worst possible rain, a slow, light rain that the cold air would freeze before it could slide off the leaves and branches, and had now made the road impossible to drive. With a sinking feeling in his gut, he looked over his shoulder at the road behind him, remembering some of the hills and curves he'd already maneuvered.

Damn it, fuck, and son of a bitch! If he'd arrived in town an hour earlier, he would've been able to make it to the Helton house and back with no problem. If he'd arrived an hour later, it would've already been impossible to make it even this far. Instead he'd arrived just in time to get his ass stuck a little more than halfway up the mountain.

Shit. He'd have to walk the rest of the way.

He switched his all-weather cap for a knit cap that he could pull down over his ears, wrestled himself into the hooded poncho his mother had given him— the Ford was a big truck, but he was a big guy, and he needed a lot of room—then tugged on his gloves. His boots were waterproof and warm, too, so at least he was dressed okay for the weather.

He grabbed the flashlight and got out of the truck, slamming the door with a vengeance, still swearing. He used all the words and variations he'd learned during his years in the army, which was a lot. Why not? No one could hear him, because everyone in their right minds was indoors, preparing for the storm. Not him. No, he had to be out in the damn storm, playing Dudley Fucking Do-Right.

He put his head down, pulled his knit cap down low to protect his ears, and tightened the drawstring of the poncho hood so the wind wouldn't blow it back. The last thing he needed was for his head to get wet. Moving to the side of the road where the narrow, weedy shoulder gave him a better surface for walking than the slick road, he plodded forward, realizing with a boulder in his gut that he was going to have to spend the night at the Helton house. No way was he getting down the mountain now, not unless he decided to walk it—and walking back to town in an ice storm would be damn near suicidal, at least right now. After the rain stopped, walking would be more feasible. Spending the night with Lolly Helton, who would probably be blindly ungrateful, was the better option . . . barely. Even then, only the thought of Sam tipped the balance toward staying.

The footing, even on the shoulder, was more precarious than he'd realized. Hell, how had he made it as far as he had without going off the road? Several times, when his feet slipped, he had to grab one of the overhanging tree limbs to keep himself upright. A sense of foreboding seized him when he played the flashlight beam along the branches and saw the layer of ice that already coated them.

At last he made it to the top of the hill. The road dipped there, then curved once again, but when he looked ahead he saw the lights of the Helton house. So, she was there after all, and hadn't made an escape earlier in the day. He didn't know if he was glad his fool's trip hadn't been in vain, or angry that he'd had to make it at all. Both, probably. He was pissed, and he intended to stay pissed.

Even though he could see the lights, the house was still almost two hundred yards away, sitting on the right in a clearing that was surrounded on three sides by the woods. Now that he was at the top, almost, he realized how much the mountain itself had been shielding him from the icy blast of wind, because it hammered at him with such force he almost staggered back. Then it eased, before another gust pounded him. Despite his layers of clothing and the poncho that kept him dry, the wind leached his body heat away and he shivered.

He'd left the two thermos bottles in the truck. Great. He'd give a lot for a cup of coffee pretty damn soon, but no way was he going back for it. He wiped the wind-blown ice crystals from his face. Maybe Lollipop would have coffee. If she did, it would probably be some flavored shit, but if it was hot he'd drink it.

That's assuming she'd let him inside.

As Gabriel neared the house he pulled his anger in, a little. A lot of years had passed since Lolly had been the spoiled stuck-up brat teenager he remembered. He wasn't the same, and she probably wouldn't be either. It wasn't her fault the sheriff was a control freak where his people were concerned. Most lawmen would've been content to assume his constituents could take care of themselves, until informed otherwise. Not Harlan McQueen.

All the lights in the downstairs appeared to be on, as was one light upstairs, in the front room on the right. There was a Mercedes SUV parked beside the front porch, and behind was an old, beat-up Blazer. He could see Lolly driving the Mercedes, but who the hell did the Blazer belong to?

Shit, maybe she had some kind of romantic rendezvous going on. What was he supposed to do now? She wouldn't want to be interrupted, and he sure as hell didn't want to do any interrupting. His only other option, though, was to walk back to the truck and spend the night there, hoping that there was enough gas in the tank to keep the truck running most of the night so he wouldn't freeze to death, at the same time praying that he—and the truck—didn't get crushed by a falling tree limb. So he guessed Lollipop would have to be pissed.

Tough shit.

Then he frowned at the two vehicles. That was weird. Why was the Mercedes parked out in an ice storm, when the garage was right there at the rear of the house? Why hadn't she parked in there, to protect her vehicle?

Instinctively he switched off his flashlight.

Before he stepped onto the porch steps, Gabriel slipped into a deep shadow and came to a dead stop. Ice danced around him, peppered his face, stuck to his coat and boots and gloves. Something wasn't right. He'd spent a long time in law enforcement, albeit the military version, and he'd learned to listen to his instincts. Right now, everything in him was telling him to approach with caution. Maybe there was nothing going on other than some screwing, but he wanted to make certain before he knocked on that door. At the very least, his dad had been wrong about Lolly being up here all alone.

Keeping to the shadows, Gabriel moved to the end of the porch and up the steps. It was an old wooden porch, and he stepped carefully, keeping to the edge of the planks where it was less likely there would be any squeaks. He didn't approach any of the windows, but shifted around until he could look past the partially open curtains into the living room where several lights burned, illuminating the man and the woman there.

The man looked as if he belonged to the truck. He was scruffy, thin, rough-looking, and dressed in clothes that bagged on him, as if he'd lost weight—either that, or they weren't his. The woman, who Gabriel could only see from behind, was painfully thin herself. Stringy dark hair fell down her back. Faded jeans bagged where her ass should be.

Lolly's hair was brown, but had she lost forty pounds, and taken up with a loser? Gabriel surveyed the rest of the room, and his gaze fell on the paraphernalia that was spread across the coffee table. *Shit!* He knew what he was looking at, and his gut tightened. If that was her, she'd started using meth, as well. No wonder she was so painfully thin.

No way in hell. His dad would have noticed something like that, known if Lolly had gotten into meth. The drug was wreaking havoc all over the country, and even in the military he had to deal with the shit. It turned users into physical wrecks, rotted their teeth out, took over their lives, and a lot of time killed them.

The man reached out to grab the woman where her ass should be, and instead of being insulted by the move, she laughed. Gabriel heard her too-loud rough laugh, as she fell back and into her companion. A hand came up and he saw the pistol she carried; it was a revolver, a big one, a .357 or even a .44. Adrenaline spurted through his veins, drastically intensifying his alertness. He didn't have a weapon with him; it hadn't even occurred to him that he'd need to come here armed.

The armed woman turned, and he stepped back enough that she wouldn't be able to see him through the window. A rush of relief filled him. The thin, wasted, angular face didn't belong to anyone he knew. Maybe it had been years since he'd seen Lolly, but no one could change that much, even on meth. That wasn't Lolly.

That didn't mean she was in the clear. Were these friends of hers? Had Lolly Helton changed in other ways, maybe not physically, but in the type of person she was? If she'd become a dealer and was caught up in this shit, he would turn around and take his chances in the truck. What else could he do? Somehow he didn't think the couple in the living room would take kindly to being interrupted. Meth users were violent, unpredictable. They'd probably shoot at him as soon as he knocked.

But where was Lolly? He couldn't leave without seeing for himself if she was okay. The Mercedes left out in the storm made him uneasy. Had these two broken in, killed her? With meth users, anything was possible, and none of it was good.

Remembering the reflected light from upstairs, he left the porch as silently as he'd stepped up, and moved back until he could see the windows. The curtains were drawn over the front window, so he circled to the side of the house. At least the curtains on that window were open. He had to move well out into the yard in order to see through the second-story window . . . and there she was.

Lolly was moving around the room, passing by the window now and then. Her face wasn't thin and wasted, like the couple downstairs, and even from here he could see that she was intent on . . . something. She pulled on a sweatshirt, even though she already wore something that looked strangely misshapen and lumpy.

As if she'd put on every piece of clothing she could find.

As if she were preparing for escape.

Gabriel took a deep breath, ignoring the cold in his lungs and the chill that surrounded him. Shit, his dad had been right. Again. Lolly *did* need rescuing.

He looked toward the detached garage. Maybe he could find a ladder in there.

Chapter Five

Every household needed a ladder, he thought, even if the house was used only a few times a year. Surely there was one around somewhere; his dad had always said Mr. Helton was a careful man, and a careful man would have a ladder. The most logical place where a careful man would put a ladder was in the garage, right? Cautiously he opened the side door into the garage, turning on the flashlight so he could see. The garage was fairly small, built in a time when most families owned only one car, and mostly empty. There were some odds and ends, some folding lawn chairs, and—*yes!*—a ladder.

He dragged it out from behind the lawn chairs, and his heart sank. This wasn't much of a ladder. For one thing, it wouldn't reach all the way to Lolly's window.

For another, it was wooden, and it was old. The rungs weren't in good shape; two were broken, and he wasn't at all sure any of the others would hold his weight. But Lolly didn't weigh as much as he did and she was the one who'd be on it, so maybe it would hold together long enough for her to climb down. If not . . . then he hoped she'd bounce. No, hell, he'd have to catch her, he thought sourly. The way his luck was running, if he didn't catch her she'd probably fall on him and break his leg, or a few ribs.

Maybe Lolly had some other way of climbing down—the old sheets-tied-together rope, for instance. If she was making preparations to escape, then she definitely had something in mind. Maybe the ladder wouldn't be needed. He sure as hell hoped not, because it was a half-rotten death trap.

But as he was hauling the ladder from the garage to the house, he looked up at the window again and saw Lolly tugging on the window frame with all her might, trying to wrest it open. She stopped, got another grip, and tried again. From what he could see the window hadn't budged an inch.

Swearing again, but this time silently, he revised his plan. He'd have to go up and raise the damn window. No matter how she'd planned to get to the ground, she wasn't going anywhere unless she could get out the window. He sent up a silent prayer. Maybe the ladder would hold together.

He had to look up to position the ladder and the icy rain felt directly on his face, in his eyes. A sudden gust of wind caught the ladder, almost tearing it from his grip. Getting the ladder propped against the house without making any noise was going to be tricky. Just in case, he mentally ran through the operation: the objective was to get up the ladder without falling and breaking his neck, open the window, get down the ladder without falling and breaking his neck, and position himself beneath the ladder so he could catch Lolly if she fell, so she wouldn't break *her* neck. Simple enough.

Oh, yeah: he had to do all that in something like five seconds flat without making any noise and alerting the two meth addicts in the living room.

No problem, he thought sarcastically. Piece of cake.

He stood the ladder up, holding it steady with both hands as he let it drop closer and closer to the house, until it settled below the window with a barely audible thunk. It must have sounded louder inside the house, though, because he saw Lolly jump back from the window as if someone had just smacked the glass. Damn it, the ladder ended a good three feet below the window casing, which meant he'd have to climb all the way to the top to have any leverage opening the window.

There was no point in delaying, so he firmly gripped the outside of the ladder and began climbing, placing his boots on the outside edges of the rungs, where they were nailed to the frame and less likely to crumble under his weight. In just a few seconds he was standing precariously on the top rung, praying like hell, and staring through the glass at Lolly Helton, who stared at him as if she couldn't decide whether to scream or faint.

She didn't do either, thank God. Instead he saw her lips move, framing his name, then she closed her eyes for a brief second before gathering herself.

When she opened her eyes again, Gabriel held a finger to his lips, signaling her to be quiet. She nodded, an obvious and telling relief washing across her face.

She'd managed to raise the window a little, after all. He worked his gloved fingers into the gap and tried to lift upward, but there was only the slightest bit of movement. The window hadn't been painted stuck, and it wasn't locked, but the old wood had warped to the point where it might as well have been. Tensing his muscles, he tried again, putting everything he had into the effort and hoping that the howl of the wind would cover the noise he made. The ladder wobbled but he ignored the precariousness of his perch and wrenched at the window again. He had to get Lolly out of the house; if he fell, then he fell. He'd deal with that when it happened.

On the third try, the window popped free and slid upward with a creaking sound. He shoved and wiggled the frame, gaining another few inches of clearance. The window wasn't all the way up, but maybe this was enough.

In a quick glance he took in the room behind her; the bed was stripped, and sure enough one end of a sheet was knotted around the leg. Then he looked at her, and for the first time saw that one side of her face was bruised and swollen. Fury roared through him, swift and deep and startlingly savage. Some asshole abusing a woman pushed all his buttons, but somehow the fact that this was Lolly hit him particularly hard. He reined in his anger, because this wasn't the time to lose control. He had to get her safely away from here; that was his primary goal. Much as he'd love to take on the jerks downstairs, they were armed and he wasn't . . . and right now the weather was damn near as dangerous as two armed, high druggies. His only concern had to be getting Lolly and himself off the mountain. Everything else could wait.

Besides, he wasn't going to recklessly put his life in danger when he had a little boy expecting his father to come home. They were probably already missing him, wondering what was taking so long.

"I saw two in the living room," he said, keeping his voice low. "Are there more?"

She shook her head. "Just those two." Her voice was as low as his.

He reached through the open window and cupped her bruised cheek in his hand; his glove was cold and wet, and it must have felt good on her face because she made a soft little moan and tilted her head against the leather. "Are you hurt anywhere else?" he asked, needing to know if she could make it down the ladder by herself. She'd been getting around okay, but adrenaline could be driving her; he'd seen people do some amazing things when they were riding an adrenaline high.

"My shoulder and side are bruised, but I'm okay," she replied in a whisper, squaring her shoulders. She added fiercely, "Let's get out of here."

She had covered as much skin as possible, he saw; even her head and her ears were lightly protected with some folded material, and a flannel shirt tied over that. She'd layered her clothing and judging by the length of sheet in her hand she was making a pretty well-planned escape. If the window hadn't been stuck, she might've been on the ground and well on her way to town by the time he'd found her.

She dropped the rope of sheets and blankets and started to put one leg out the window. "Wait," he said, thinking fast. If she tossed the rope out the window and left it hanging, and he put the ladder away after she was down, the assholes downstairs would believe she'd made it out on her own. That way if they were stupid enough to get out in the storm and come after her, they'd be caught by surprise if—or when—they discovered that she was not alone. Just as swiftly he disregarded the plan, because the bottom sheet would be flapping right in front of the dining room window, and might alert them sooner than necessary. He was holding his breath hoping they didn't see the ladder through the window; at least the aged wood was dark, and not as easily made out as a white sheet would be.

He surveyed Lolly once more. She'd done the best

she could to dress warmly, but the rain would seep right through all those layers, and then she'd be in deep trouble.

Moving carefully, the rickety ladder wobbling under him, Gabriel removed his poncho and handed it through the window. Lolly took it, then gave him a sharp look. "What about you?"

"You need it more. At least my coat is weatherproof." The poncho was covered with ice crystals, but provided much better protection against the rain than what she was wearing. His coat was heavy, he had gloves, and his feet were protected by warm, waterproof boots. The only problem was that the knit cap he wore wasn't waterproof, like the cap he'd discarded in the truck, but he hadn't known then he'd be giving the hooded poncho to Lolly. The knit would repel the rain for a while, but eventually his head was going to get wet, and that wasn't good. When they got to the truck he'd retrieve his cap; he could make it that far without too much risk of hypothermia.

"I'm going back down," he whispered. "This ladder is half rotten, and it won't hold both of us at the same time." He wasn't certain it would stay together long enough for him to get down, but if it didn't, they'd go back to plan A and the tied-together sheets. "There are two broken rungs. One is halfway down, the other is three below it. Put your feet on the outside of the rungs, not in the middle."

Lolly nodded, and began pulling on the poncho over her layers of clothing. Gabriel carefully backed down the ladder, not taking a deep breath until his boots were safely on the icy ground again. He turned up the collar of his jacket to protect his neck from the wind, and positioned himself so he could brace the ladder. She stuck her head out to make certain he was on the ground, then quickly drew it back in and stuck one leg out the window, feeling with her foot for the top rung. She couldn't reach it, of course, because the ladder wasn't tall enough. Finally she sat on the windowsill, put both legs out, and turned until she was on her stomach. She found the ladder, set both feet on it, and cautiously moved down the creaking wood. She was favoring her right side, he noticed, and wondered how she'd hold up for the long hike off the mountain.

The walk, which would be treacherous because of the ice, would take hours. In normal circumstances he wouldn't even attempt it, but the circumstances weren't normal and the only other choice they had was to simply hide and wait . . . but wait for what? The meth addicts in the living room were stuck, too; they weren't going anywhere, and at least they were in a warm house. He and Lolly couldn't wait for the ice to melt, because that could take a week or more. Their best bet, and it wasn't a good one, but it was better than their other options, was to get off the mountain as fast as they could, before the weight of the ice started snapping tree limbs like toothpicks. They'd be warmer if they were moving, too.

"Watch for that missing rung," he warned in an urgent whisper just before she reached it, and her step faltered. She hesitated, then changed her rhythm and instead used her right foot to step past the missing rung, so she could bear most of her weight with her left shoulder instead of the bruised right one.

A splintering sound was the only warning he had, before the next rung gave way, too, and she came tumbling down.

It wasn't a long drop, but in these conditions and with the hike they had ahead of them, a sprained ankle was as good as a broken leg. Instinctively Gabriel let go of the ladder and grabbed Lolly in a bear hug before she could hit the ground. The ladder clattered and banged against the side of the house.

"Shit!" he said, setting Lolly on her feet and grabbing her wrist. There was almost no chance the two inside hadn't heard the ladder slamming against the house. They needed to move—*now.*

"Let's go," he said, and started across the icy yard at a fast clip, towing her behind him. She didn't make a sound of protest, just put her head down and did her best to keep up. They slipped and slid, but he kept his feet; once Lolly started sliding, but she regained her balance, aided by his grip on her wrist. If they could just make the tree line . . .

There was a shout behind them, and a shot rang out.

Double shit.

Chapter Six

Lolly went down with a cry of pain, and for one stark split-second time froze as Gabriel thought she'd been shot. Then she was scrambling to her feet, muttering "Damn it!" with muffled fury before grabbing his hand and taking off again. She fell again, almost immediately; the thick treads on his boots didn't afford him a lot of traction, but her sneakers had almost none.

Gabriel hauled her to her feet once more; she stifled another cry of pain, and too late he realized he'd pulled on her right arm, and her injured right shoulder. To keep her upright, he wrapped his arm around her and held her, his grip so hard he expected her to protest, but she didn't make a peep. Running in that locked-together position was impossible, unless they wanted to end up facedown on the ground while the two meth-heads took potshots at them. Their best bet was to keep moving, no matter how agonizingly slow their progress seemed to be.

At least it was dark up here, away from the lights of town and other houses; hiding would be easier. Of course, that meant they had to be extra cautious themselves, because he couldn't turn on the flashlight without pinning a bull's-eye on their backs. All he could do was keep moving, get them into the trees, and hope for the best.

Even though she'd spent the last hour—two hours? She had no idea how much time had passed—in terror, expecting to be killed, somehow the first explosive crack of a gunshot still caught Lolly by surprise; her entire body lurched, and her heart jumped so hard it felt as if it would come out of her chest. She stumbled, lost her balance on the icy grass, and went down. Cold immediately seared her legs. The poncho somewhat protected her, but from mid-thigh down her pants were wet. After all the effort she'd made to stay dry, what did she do but fall on the wet ground the very first thing? Furious with herself, she scrambled up, grabbed Gabriel's hand, and took off running again.

And immediately fell again.

This time Gabriel jerked her to her feet, and the

pressure on her bruised shoulder and side wrenched a cry from her before she stubbornly shut her mouth. What was a little pain in her shoulder compared to maybe getting shot? Gabriel clamped his arm around her waist and set off again, all but dragging her along with him.

Behind them, the porch light flared on, and the front door opened with a pop and a slam; the first shot must have been through the dining room window if they were just now making it out on the porch. Niki and Darwin began firing from the porch; their aim was off, but every cell in her spinal cord seemed to shrivel as she waited for a lucky shot to find her. Again, time seemed to have lost its meaning; logically only ten or fifteen seconds could have passed, because how long could it have taken them to get to the porch? It felt as if she and Gabriel had been running for the woods for a lifetime, but they were still several yards away. Lolly was afraid to turn and look at the porch, afraid to do anything except try to keep her feet under her and make as much progress as she could.

Don't fall, don't fall. Instinct screamed at her to run, but even with Gabriel's support it was all she could do to keep her feet under her. They were still on grass, which wasn't nearly as slick as the driveway would be, but every step sent her feet slipping and skating in various directions. Gabriel fared better, maybe because of his boots, maybe because he was heavier and crunched through the layer of ice to the ground. *Don't fall.* She clutched the back of his coat in a death grip, hanging on for dear life.

Then they reached the tree line and Gabriel whirled, shoving her behind one of the larger trees and pressing himself full against her as if he were trying to push her into the rough bark. Lolly clung to him, her head buried against his shoulder as she sucked in huge, rapid gulps of air. Random shots splintered the air, the sound curiously flat and muffled, as if it was absorbed by the ice instead of echoing back. Her heart still pounded like something wild, even though they were significantly safer behind this tree trunk than they had been before. But what now? If they ran, they'd be exposed again, at least sporadically. If they didn't run, then all Niki and Darwin had to do was walk across the yard to shoot them at close range.

Gabriel incrementally leaned to the left, until he could see the house but still presented almost no target, given they were in the darkness of the tree line and Niki and Darwin were hampered by standing on a lighted porch. Even knowing they likely couldn't see a thing, Lolly's hands involuntarily tightened on Gabriel's coat as she tried to wrench him back to safety. She couldn't move him at all, not even a fraction of an inch.

His right hand patted her shoulder, the movement so absent she knew the reassuring gesture was pure reflex. He was concentrating on the situation, on the two murderous idiots on the front porch. Feeling slightly ashamed for being such a wuss, Lolly forced herself to release him. She'd gotten this far without turning into a spineless blob; she'd make it the rest of the way, or die trying . . . literally.

"How many weapons did you see?" He breathed the words, the sound barely existent.

"Two." That didn't mean there weren't more, though. For all she knew, there was a cache of weapons in their old Blazer.

"Do you know guns?" he asked.

She shook her head. She knew what a shotgun looked like, because her dad had gone skeet shooting, but her experience was limited to that and whatever she'd seen on television or in a movie.

"Can you tell the difference between a revolver and an automatic?"

That much she did know. "They were both automatics . . . I think. I didn't get a good look at the one he had." Darwin had pulled it from his pocket, but she'd barely had time to register the fact before he'd shoved her against the newel post.

"I don't suppose you could tell me how many bullets they had in each gun," he said wryly.

Lolly just shook her head, even though the question had been rhetorical. Had he actually been *counting* the number of shots? She'd barely been able to think at all, much less keep track of how many shots were being fired.

Then the gunshots stopped, and that was almost

more frightening than being shot at. What was happening? Were Niki and Darwin coming after them? She could hear the two of them yelling at each other. She could also hear her own heartbeat, Gabriel's breathing, and the wind. At this moment, there was nothing else.

"What are we going to do now?" she whispered. Her voice was all but lost against his thick coat, but Gabriel heard her and gave her another of those absent pats.

"We're going down the mountain. There's nothing else we can do, no other option." He didn't sound happy about that, but she couldn't think of anything else they could do, either. She'd been prepared to make her way down the mountain alone, anyway, so she wasn't going to complain.

Gabriel looked toward the house, took Lolly's hand again, and together they eased away from their protected position behind the tree to move deeper into the woods. His step was quick but sure, and she had to struggle a little to keep pace. Her legs weren't as long as his, and hiking through the woods wasn't exactly her thing. She didn't have many "things," she realized. She was excruciatingly normal, lived a normal life, worked at a normal job. She liked books and movies, forced herself to exercise, but despite growing up in Maine, she didn't care for roughing it or any winter sports at all, so she was definitely out of her element right now.

The trees had sheltered the ground beneath them,

so there was less ice here, though their feet still made crunching sounds. That meant ice was building on the limbs and branches overhead, and she knew how dangerous that could be; working for an insurance company had given her insight into all sorts of situations, because she'd seen the claims.

Gabriel led her at an angle that generally followed the long driveway toward the narrow secondary road, stepping over fallen dead branches, maneuvering around clumps of wild growth. A couple of times he looked back at her. She felt like a tethered balloon, being tugged along in his wake. Her breath huffed out in rapid gasps. He must have realized that she was struggling to keep up with him because he shortened his stride, but not by much. "It'll be a bit easier when we can leave the woods," he said once, as he helped her around an overgrown, brambly bush. "I have soup and coffee in my truck."

"Dangling a carrot, eh?"

That might've been a smile, but it was so dark she couldn't be sure. "Whatever works."

"Um . . . exactly where *is* your truck?" The shock had worn off enough now that she could think a little. Obviously Gabriel hadn't flown there, so he had to have wheels somewhere.

"About half a mile farther. The ice was so bad I had to stop."

Questions tumbled in her mind, questions like: why was he here? It wasn't as if she and Gabriel McQueen were close friends—or even *friends,* come to that. Of all the people in the world, what was *he* doing at her house? None of this felt real, and somehow his presence was the most unreal part of it all. Being knocked around, terrorized, almost raped, and held captive were all shocking enough in their own right, but the fact that he, of all people, had appeared out of the night to help her escape was simply dumbfounding— either that, she thought wryly, or this was her brain's way of helping her cope by shoving all that other stuff to the side until she could cope.

If concentrating on Gabriel McQueen was a coping mechanism, then she'd go along with the game plan; that was much better than thinking of the violence, of everything that could go wrong, of how dangerous walking for miles in weather like this could be. The odds were so heavy against them surviving the night that only sheer desperation made her willing to try.

The darkness in the woods was almost complete; they both stumbled over obstacles, feeling their way along. Her eyes had adjusted somewhat, and still she could barely see. If Gabriel had a flashlight he didn't produce it, and she didn't ask; much as she wanted to see where she was going, she seriously didn't want the equivalent of a spotlight pinpointing their position for Niki and Darwin.

In spite of the poncho Gabriel had given her, before long the cold cut through all the layers of clothing she wore. Her jeans and sweatpants were wet from falling on the ice, and the wind went right through to her skin. She would have liked nothing better than to stop and hunker down so the poncho draped around her and blocked the wind, but if she stopped moving she was afraid she wouldn't be able to start up again. Knowing what waited behind her, in the warmth of her own home, spurred her to keep up. She'd walk all the way to Portland if that was what it took to get away from those two.

She'd even put her life in the hands of Gabriel McQueen, who had been the bane of her teenage years. He'd been everything she wasn't: popular, out-going, self-assured. And she'd had the most horribly painful crush on him all through junior high and high school. The flip side of that was she'd hated him, too, for all the times he'd made fun of her, all the times he'd taunted her and laughed at her, and she'd never passed up an opportunity to slip a verbal knife between his ribs. When he'd graduated two years ahead of her, she'd been relieved, yet she'd still caught herself watching the hallways for that proudly held dark head.

She should probably count herself lucky he'd bothered rescuing her. The teenage Gabriel wouldn't have bothered—though, to be fair, if she'd still been a teenager she'd probably have slammed the window on his hands anyway.

Thinking about the past could occupy her mind only so long before her physical misery began to push its way to the forefront. The rain was coming down harder now, coating the trees, the underbrush, even them. She couldn't see it, but she could feel the weight of it crusting her wet pants and shoes. At least her feet didn't seem to be quite as wet as her legs, thanks to the Vaseline . . . either that, or they were so cold she couldn't feel the moisture. The wind soughed through the tree limbs, making them rattle like bones in their ice-coffins. The sound was eerie, ghostly, and she was glad for the big, hard hand that gripped hers.

Then Gabriel pushed through some particularly heavy undergrowth and halted so abruptly she plowed into his back. "Finally," he said, reaching back to steady her. "Here's the road. There's about a three-foot drop down to it, so be careful."

He bent down, gripped a sapling, and used it to steady himself as he jumped down the low embankment. His feet skidded on the ice, but with the aid of the sapling he stayed upright. Gingerly he turned, reached up, and grasped Lolly around the waist, then lowered her to the road with easy strength. "Watch your step," he warned. "There's a shallow ditch here. Walk on the weedy strip between the ditch and the pavement; it's better footing."

Head down, Lolly concentrated on putting one foot in front of the other. Surely they had gone more than a half mile; shouldn't they have reached his truck by now? She had grown up on this mountain, knew it like the back of her hand, most of the time, but the darkness, the cold, the unrelenting series of shocks, had all left her disoriented and she had no real idea where they were. Her hands and feet hurt so much from the cold she felt as if she could barely shuffle forward. She couldn't do anything about her feet, and Gabriel gripped one of her hands so she couldn't do anything about it, either, but her other hand she wormed under the poncho and several other layers of clothing to reach the bare skin of her warm belly. She could barely feel the warmth on her fingers, but her belly could definitely feel the cold of her hand. There, that was a little better.

Now and then she darted a glance at the man who was leading her, though in the darkness she couldn't make out much more than his height and the width of his shoulders—that, and the determination with which he faced the storm head-on. She remembered the way he'd looked when he'd popped up in her window, though. He was older, obviously; so was she. A lot of years had passed since he'd graduated—fifteen of them!—and they'd both changed.

He was no longer a cocky teenager with the world at his feet; he was a grown man, a widower with a son, as she'd heard during one of her trips to Wilson Creek. Becoming a father and losing his wife were life-changing events; no way could he be the same person he was when they were in school. She wasn't, and she hadn't been through anything as traumatic as losing a spouse. There was nothing traumatic in her life at all. Instead she'd quietly made her way, made a settled life for herself, shed a lot of her insecurities and shyness.

She had butted heads with him for as long as she

could remember, and right now . . . she wasn't sure why. Was it because she'd always had such a ferocious crush on him, and never expected him to like her in any way, so she'd protected herself by developing a shield of hostility? Teenagers were such tangled pits of angst and emotion, anything was possible. Looking back, she felt slightly bemused by their teenage selves.

If there would ever be any time for putting the past behind them, that time was now. She leaned slightly toward him and said, "Thank you," her voice raised so he could hear her over the rain and the wind.

"Thank me if those psychos don't come after us and we get off the mountain before the trees start to fall," he said without looking at her.

Okay, that sounded a little abrupt, but she did something that, fifteen years ago, she could never have done: she mentally shrugged and let it go. Under the circumstances, he was allowed to feel testy.

They were walking right into the wind now, which gave her some bearings. Lolly glanced up, but not for long; the rain stung her face like icy pellets, the wind stole her breath with its chill. The wind was from the north, so if it was in her face then they were walking north, which meant they were on the long slope before a very sharp curve that would take them southeast.

They weren't that far from the house at all.

They had some time before the ice that coated everything was so heavy these old trees started to come down . . . she hoped. How long would the dead trees hold up with this wind and ice? she wondered. Their fragile limbs would come down first. The side of the road was littered with limbs that had fallen in one storm or another and been left to lie, giving her a hint as to the length and breadth of what might come crashing down.

The wind picked up a bit just then and the trees creaked, literally, as if their very fabric was groaning. Lolly shuddered. They had one option, and it wasn't a good one. Darwin and Niki were behind them, ice-covered limbs hovered above their heads and could come crashing down at any time, and the ground was increasingly slick beneath her feet. There was no place to go except forward, toward the safety and warmth that seemed so very far away.

She slipped, her sneakers giving her no purchase at all. The Vaseline definitely helped, but some moisture had seeped into her shoes and socks and her feet were painfully numb. She'd grown up in Maine; she knew the dangers of frostbite. She knew what the outcome of the night was likely to be, and a sense of fatalism seized her. Better to lose her toes than let herself get caught by Darwin again.

She adjusted the sleeves of the flannel shirt tied over her head, pulling them over her nose and mouth, but the sleeves were wet and icy and she didn't know if that would do much good. Thank goodness Gabriel was there, steady as a rock, plowing forward with the determination of a pit bull. His grip was solid, a comfort in a decidedly uncomfortable world. He was that kind of man, she supposed, the kind who would go out in an ice storm to make sure a neighbor was all right, a man who would throw himself between danger and a woman even if she was nothing to him, even if she was a girl he'd once known and hadn't liked.

She hadn't had a chance to tell him everything that had happened back at the house and after a moment of reflection she decided she wouldn't. Not only did she not want to talk about Darwin's attempted rape, she wasn't sure how Gabriel would react to the news. Would he feel as if he had to turn back? Would he care at all? She suspected he would care, just because of who he was, and she didn't want to go back to the house. She didn't want Gabriel going back there either, and for now she was sticking by his side. Her sights were set firmly away from the house and the nightmare there. No matter what the conditions, she was moving forward.

There was silence behind them—at least human silence. Mother Nature was making a racket, with the patter of falling rain, the wind, the ghostly rustling and creaking of the trees. Maybe they'd given up. Maybe they hadn't given chase at all. Maybe Niki and Darwin were unwilling to leave a nice warm house in this weather, just to chase her and Gabriel.

She glanced up once more, at the tall man towing her along. "So . . . how've you been?" she asked.

Gabriel snorted. "You want to chitchat now?"

"Maybe talking will keep my face from freezing."

He nodded once. "I've been okay. You?"

So much for dragging him into conversation. "Fine." What else could she say? *Still single. Job's good, if unexciting. Mom and Dad are in good health, but they lost a good bit of their retirement money in the latest financial disaster, so keeping a house they no longer use is ridiculous. I didn't want to sell it, but I can't afford to buy it from them, and now I don't want to. I loved that house, and now I don't care if I never see it again.* The sense of loss was surprisingly sharp; she took it in, accepted that she would never again feel the same about the house, then she resolutely put the house in the past where it belonged and mentally faced forward.

She should have been paying attention to what she was doing, rather than wool-gathering. She slipped again, and once more Gabriel caught her.

"We need to get you out of this ice," he said, his tone concerned. She had to admit, getting out of the weather was a good idea. The best, in fact. But there wasn't a neighbor for miles, and town was even farther.

"My truck isn't far," he added encouragingly.

Lolly knew very well that these roads were now impassible. Nasty as it was, dangerous as it was, she'd rather walk down the steep road than get in a vehicle and take the chance of slipping and sliding over the side of the mountain. There were some wicked curves and steep drop-offs between here and Wilson Creek. But they could stop at Gabriel's truck, get inside and get warm, maybe break out the soup and coffee. With that thought in mind, she had a reasonable destination in mind and that kept her moving forward, putting one foot in front of the other. If she had to think of walking all the way down the mountain she'd probably drop here and now, certain she couldn't make it.

None of this was real. It couldn't be. Her life was unexciting, boring, ordinary. To fight off an attack, escape through a second-story window, get shot at and fight against a storm as dangerous as what she'd left behind—these were things she'd never thought to do. Lolly decided she liked unexciting. At the moment, she craved it. She'd never again complain about being bored. This . . . this was all like a bad dream.

Every step now was a struggle. The cold cut through her clothes, slowing her down. Her instincts screamed at her to stop, rest, give in, but she knew if she stopped here, she'd die. Freezing to death couldn't be a pleasant way to go, and even if it was, she wasn't ready to go.

"Soup," Lolly said with all-but-frozen lips, throwing the word out like a talisman, something to keep her going. Suddenly she realized she was starving. The thought of the soup warming her from the inside out encouraged her to keep moving, even when the ground beneath her turned sharply down and each step became even more precarious.

"Yes, there's soup." His arm was tighter around her now; he was all but carrying her. Lolly gathered her strength, focused on what she was doing.

If she could just get some soup—and coffee! He'd

said he had coffee!—she'd be able to make it. They could rest for a few minutes, turn the truck heater on full blast and thaw out a little, have some soup and coffee, and be on their way. With a little fortification, she'd be good to go.

Then there was an enraged shout from above, followed by a gunshot, and terror blasted its way through every fiber of her body. Darwin was coming for her after all.

Chapter Seven

Darwin followed Niki out onto the porch, reluctant to leave the comfort of the house. The wind was brutal out here, and . . . hell, was that *ice*? The shit covered everything, even the Blazer. He hadn't noticed any ice when they'd been out here just a little while ago, after the Lorelei bitch went out the second-story window and escaped. He blamed Niki for that. If she'd just left them alone, everything would have been okay. He'd have had some fun, and Lorelei wouldn't have been in any shape to go out the window. Now that strange dude who'd showed up out of nowhere would be the one having the fun.

Man, that ice was unreal. He thought it might have been sleeting before, but to come outside and find everything coated with ice was fucking weird.

He scratched at his face, and thought he needed another hit of meth. They still had plenty inside, unless that bitch Niki had used it all. She was using more than her fair share, he thought resentfully. She was always doing that, and he was tired of it. Yeah, she was good about coming up with ideas for getting more money, but then she used up the shit so it was her fault they had to have more money, anyway.

"It's your fault," he said, because he was tired of her bitching and complaining and the way she wanted to make all the decisions. He stared at the icicles hanging from the eaves of the porch. This was her fault, too, because she'd come up with the bright idea of following Lorelei home, when they could have taken her money in town and wouldn't be stuck on this fucking mountain now. "If you hadn't left her alone upstairs, she wouldn't have got away."

Niki erupted in rage. "That bitch!" she screamed, and fired a shot at Lorelei's Mercedes, which might have made her feel better but was a waste of a bullet, as far as Darwin was concerned. Was the stupid car going to feel anything? They didn't have many bullets left, he figured, after all the shooting they'd done earlier. They'd gone back inside and Niki had spent the time working herself into a fit, but neither of them had checked how many rounds were left in the guns. Then Niki decided they had to go look for Lorelei and insisted they come outside, made him put on his coat and get a flashlight, but Darwin had lost all his enthusiasm for that. Niki could go out in this shit if she wanted to; he was going back inside.

"You'll pay for this!" Niki screeched into the night, as if Lorelei was standing around out there listening to her. She turned to face Darwin, her face twisted and distorted, her sunken eyes glaring at him. "When we find Lorelei and kill the bastard with her, I'm going to let you have her. That'll teach the bitch to play games with me!"

Now, that sounded interesting. Darwin's spirits lifted as he regained his enthusiasm. "Really?"

"As long as you let me watch and you make it hurt, why not? Teach her to fuck with me," Niki added beneath her breath.

Okay, maybe that was worth going out in the weather for. Lorelei . . . women like her looked down their noses at him. It would be nice to have someone like her to do what he wanted to, to treat any way he liked. Yeah, that would be fun. Maybe he'd keep her. Maybe he'd get rid of Niki and train Lorelei right. A dose or two of meth and she'd be begging for it, willing to do anything he told her so long as he kept giving the ice to her.

They had found several flashlights in the house and each carried one: a gun in one hand, a flashlight in the other. Carefully they made their way down the steps, and Darwin grabbed the door handle of the Blazer.

"Don't be stupid, Stupid," Niki snapped. "If they're

hiding in the woods and we're driving along in the Blazer, how the hell we gonna see them? Unless they're dumb enough to be standing in the middle of the road, we won't. They're on foot, so we have to be on foot."

She called *him* stupid? he thought, the resentment bubbling again. He wasn't the one who let Lorelei get away in the first place.

He trained the beam of his flashlight down the driveway. The ray of light cut the darkness, but didn't exactly illuminate the area for them. It was too dark and the flashlights weren't all that great; they'd be fine for finding his way around a house if the power went out, but they weren't a whole lot of good for a manhunt. Still, they were better than nothing. Lorelei and her pal had to be down there somewhere, and they weren't armed. If they had been they would've fired back as they'd been making their escape. They were probably hiding, waiting until they thought he and Niki had gone to sleep before they snuck back into the house. Only reason anyone would stay out in this mess was if they had no choice.

He'd shoot the guy on sight, get him out of the way, then there wouldn't be any way for Lorelei to escape. His imagination took over, and he remembered how pretty and soft she was, how good she felt. Without watching what he was doing, Darwin took a step and his foot shot out from under him. He hit the ground ass first and the flashlight went flying, but he managed to hold on to his gun. The impact rattled his bones, stole his breath. Niki, damn her, bent over laughing.

"Get on the side of the road, you moron," she said, shining the beam from her flashlight into his face and effectively blinding him. Great. Now he wouldn't be able to see anything at all for a while.

Darwin slowly rose to his feet, edging off the driveway and onto the grassy shoulder. Once he was there, he retrieved his flashlight and a portion of his dignity. He looked down the slope, imagining the woman he craved to the bone hiding there, somewhere. He'd make her pay for this. He didn't let Niki know how much his ass hurt, because he knew she'd make fun of him if she knew. Niki had a mean streak in her, and she didn't care who she turned it on.

Well, fuck her. No, forget that. He'd rather fuck Lorelei. Get rid of Niki, take Lorelei instead.

"Oh, Lorelei," he called in a singsong voice. "Where are you, Lorelei? Come 'ere, baby, come to daddy."

Niki laughed again. She was easily amused tonight, flipping from rage to laughter at the slightest reason. They eased down the slope. The icy wind blew the stinging rain into his eyes. His ass hurt. They were chasing after two people who had a head start, in the dark, but at the moment he didn't much care about any of that. Lorelei was going to pay for running away from them.

He remembered her expression of terror when

he'd had her down on the kitchen floor. He'd liked that, liked the feeling of power, of knowing he could make her so scared she'd been about to pass out. Yeah, he'd like having her around for a while. He'd like showing her how ice could make her feel, like having her beg him for it—and for anything else he wanted to give her. "I think I want her high this time," he said as he took careful steps down the hill. If she was high she'd like what he gave her, whether she wanted to or not.

"You hold her down, I'll shoot her up," Niki said, then, like a light switch flipping, went straight into anger again. "The damn bitch!"

"Works for me." Reckless with anticipation, Darwin tried to hurry. His foot slipped again and his arms windmilled until he got his balance. Cursing, he slowed down. He'd better not fall; he might break something he'd need later. Snickering, he called out again. "Lorelei! Ready or not, here I come." He laughed at his own pun—and Niki thought he was stupid.

Gabriel reacted immediately at the flat crack of the gunshot, pushing Lolly up the embankment, back into the woods. A quick glance showed the flashlight beams dancing as the druggies came down the hill, not nearly as far away as he'd like. They hadn't been forced to cut through the woods but had gone straight from the house to the driveway, which had saved them time. They weren't more than fifty yards away.

Fortunately, they couldn't move any faster than he and Lolly could. Unfortunately, they could use their flashlights and they were armed. If they shone their lights into the woods at the right place at the right time, and they were halfway decent shots, he and Lolly would be sitting ducks.

In this weather, hunkering down in the woods wasn't a great idea. They needed to keep moving so they didn't get too cold, but at the same time movement would give away their location. He just hoped tree limbs didn't start snapping.

He found a big pine and positioned Lolly behind it, concealing her as best he could between his body and the tree trunk. He bent his head so his mouth was close to her ear. "After they go past, we're going to backtrack. They won't expect it, and we can hide in the garage until morning."

She nodded, her head moving against his shoulder. Gabriel hoped he wasn't making a mistake. He'd have liked to get to the truck, get some hot coffee, get this frozen knit cap off his head. He was losing so much body heat through his head that he wasn't certain how much longer he could keep going, but he didn't want to say anything to Lolly. He didn't want her feeling guilty because she had his poncho. It wasn't her fault two brain-fried meth addicts were hunting them down; none of this was her fault.

"If we're lucky, they'll break their fool necks long

before then." He wouldn't mind at all. He'd leave their bodies where they lay, and get himself and Lolly back to the house as fast as they could move.

Again, Lolly nodded.

Of course, they hadn't had a lot of luck so far tonight; what were the odds they'd get lucky now?

In the wood behind them, he heard the crackle of wood straining to resist the weight of the ice, and the sound sent a shiver down his back that had nothing to do with the cold and everything to do with dread. Lolly heard it, too. Her head lifted, and he felt the stillness in her body as she listened, waiting. It was early in the storm for limbs to start falling, but when he took into account the number of dead trees in these woods and the wind that would make the limbs fall sooner, he knew they didn't have long. The question was, how soon would limbs start to drop, and how widespread would the fall be?

Dead limbs first; healthy limbs later. Then treetops would be splintering and falling; by morning entire trees would be coming down. If they didn't get off the mountain soon, they weren't going anywhere for a while.

"Lorelei! Ready or not, here I come!"

Lolly shuddered in his arms as she heard the lilting, savagely amused voice of the man who'd invaded her home. Gabriel didn't like the way the man called her name, didn't like the way Lolly trembled. She hadn't given him any details about what had happened before he'd arrived—there hadn't been time—

but he knew how violent meth addicts could be. Whatever had happened—and he'd find out later, *if* they survived—she was handling it.

He'd never thought he would be admiring of Lolly Helton, but damn if he wasn't. Not only had she showed plenty of spunk and common sense, not once had she complained, though he knew her feet had to be excruciatingly cold in those inadequate sneakers. A lot of people, with perfect justification, would have been ready to sit down and give up, but Lolly just put her head down and kept going. Given that determination, *something* had to have happened to make her react to the meth-head like this.

He tightened his arms around her, offering her both protection and comfort. "I won't let him hurt you," he breathed, because the two addicts were closer now and even a low tone would be too loud. That was a promise he intended to keep, come hell or high water, unless he was dead. Grimly he assessed the situation. If the two would pass by, keep going, and get far enough away that he and Lolly could make it back up the hill again without drawing attention to themselves . . . there had to be something in the garage he could use as a weapon, if it came to a confrontation.

Lolly leaned forward, fell into him. Her arms went around his waist, held him tight. They had on too many clothes to share any body heat, but the contact was nice. Gabriel gently cupped the back of her head, held her to his shoulder. All they had to do now was be very still and very quiet, and pray they weren't seen. If they could just stay here a while longer, if they could melt into the darkness and be invisible . . .

Soon the druggies were too close for even an exchange of a whisper. He felt tension coiling in her muscles, but she didn't move an inch. Even over the wind, he could hear the two talking as they picked their way down the hill, occasionally shining their flashlights into the woods. The flashlights were standard household models, the beams weak compared to what he used, but he and Lolly were just barely inside the tree line and the lights easily penetrated that far. He kept his face tucked down, because the relative paleness of bare skin was almost like a beacon in the dark.

The change from just a couple of hours ago was staggering. When he'd left his parents' house Gabriel had expected to do battle with the weather and with Lolly, but this . . . this had never crossed his mind.

A beam of light flashed just a few feet to his right. The tree they stood behind gave them some cover, but not enough, not with light coming in from an angle. If they moved in order to keep the tree between them and the druggies, they'd make too much noise. There were twigs, untended undergrowth, and even dead leaves left to rot from the autumn fall—not to mention the ice—all at their feet. Even with the wind howling, it was more likely that movement would alert the hunters to their hiding place than their intermittent flashlight beams would find them.

Lolly stopped breathing. So did he. And as luck—very bad luck—would have it, a beam of light caught his sleeve. He watched it from the corner of his eye, watched it move away, then suddenly return and settle on his face. A woman's voice yelled, "I got 'em! Darwin! Over here!"

No point in keeping quiet now. Gabriel shoved Lolly away from the tree, away from the flashlight, and lunged for deeper cover. "Run," he said, grabbing her arm, and they both ran like hell as a gunshot exploded behind them.

Niki aimed into the woods where she'd seen the man, his face a startling bit of white in the darkness, and fired, but she was too slow. The two disappeared, but she could hear them crashing deeper into the woods. She'd lose them in there, and she didn't like letting anyone get away from her, especially some hoity-toity rich bitch like Lorelei. She fired again, her aim following the sound they made as they ran. This was like hunting, she thought in pleased excitement as she followed them into the woods. Lorelei Helton and her friend were just like deer, a doe and a buck, running from danger, running from her gun. She liked thinking they were frantic with fear, and completely defenseless.

"Don't shoot the woman!" Darwin shouted with what seemed to be real concern in his voice.

"Like I can see what I'm shooting at," Niki screamed.

The bastard, all he wanted was the woman. He was really good at just sitting on his ass and letting her do all the work, then telling her how to do it. She'd do better without him, and maybe, just maybe, the day was coming when she'd do something about that. Right now, though, she had to track some deer. She moved forward, her footing sturdier once she was entirely under the trees. She picked up the pace then, continuing in the direction she'd heard her deer take, sweeping her hand from side to side and pulling the trigger until the hammer just made a clicking sound and there were no more bullets left. On her right, Darwin was shooting, too, finally more concerned about not letting the two get away than he was about wounding or killing his prize.

Neither of them were trained shooters. Even on a good day, all they could do was point and pull the trigger; it wasn't like they usually cared if they hit anything or not. Just the fear of a weapon, the fear of getting shot, was usually enough to make people do what they wanted, and when they did shoot someone it was always up close where there was no question of missing. They'd never before needed more than a bullet or two, maybe three, to get what they wanted.

Within seconds, Darwin was out of ammunition himself. They stopped, unsure what to do now. They flicked their flashlight beams around, but couldn't see anything other than black tree trunks, underbrush, and ice. Well, wasn't this great? Here they were, standing in the woods, cold, angry, and effectively disarmed. To top it off, that bitch Lorelei had gotten away again. While there were plenty of sounds in the forest, none seemed to be coming from the human deer.

A tickle of warning crawled up Niki's spine. Without bullets she didn't feel nearly as confident as she had just moments ago. Maybe this hadn't been such a good idea. Besides, she was coming down from the last hit, and she needed another one pretty soon. She'd feel better then.

"Forget it," she said angrily. "We'll go back to the house and get warm, and in the morning when the sun comes up and melts the ice on the road, we can get out of here."

"But what about Lorelei?" Darwin asked, whining like a kid who'd just dropped his ice-cream cone in the sand.

Niki tamped down her surge of jealousy. "Your bitch Lorelei and her friend are going to freeze to death out there." With her useless gun, she gestured into the depths of the forest. It was so dark, and shit, now that the hunt had lost its appeal, the cold was starting to really seep through her coat.

"But . . ."

"You want to keep looking? Fine. Go right ahead. I'm going back to the house and I'm going to enjoy myself."

"Just five more minutes of looking around and—" There was a faint rustle behind them. Darwin went still. The beam from his flashlight danced across the dark forest floor. "Did you hear that?"

Too late, Niki said, "Turn off that light!" She fumbled with cold gloved hands to press the switch on the one she carried to the off position, but it was too late. In the beam of Darwin's flashlight, she saw the long, thick tree limb that came swinging from behind, like a baseball bat aimed at the side of his head.

Chapter Eight

Gabriel pulled them to a halt behind yet another big tree. "Stay here, and don't move a muscle," he whispered.

He moved away from her and she almost lunged to grab his jacket and hold him back. She didn't deliberately go toward danger, she ran away from it; that's what made sense to her. But Gabriel was military, and his training was not only to go to the danger, but to neutralize it. Her heart jumped into her throat and lodged there, knowing he was risking his life. Every instinct in her screamed for her to stop him, beg him not to leave her, to hold him there and keep him as safe as possible.

She bit her lip until the sharp coppery taste of

blood touched her tongue. She had to do exactly as he said, or she'd be endangering him even more.

Gabriel stooped slowly and silently, his hands sweeping the ground around him. He picked up an old fallen limb that was about three feet long and hefted it, then silently discarded it and began feeling for another one. Lolly tried to keep an eye on Darwin and Niki for him, so she could warn him if they got closer. They had stopped, and from the sharpness of their voices, appeared to be arguing, though she couldn't make out any individual words. She glanced back at Gabriel, and he was gone.

In a panic she looked in all directions, but she couldn't see him. He had disappeared into the rain and darkness.

But if she couldn't see him, then likely Darwin and Niki wouldn't be able to either . . . except for those damn flashlights. Maybe she could draw their attention her way— No. She discarded the idea as soon as it formed. Gabriel had told her not to move. If she did, not only would he not have any idea where she was, in the darkness he wouldn't be able to tell her from the bad guys. Gabriel McQueen was hunting, and she didn't want to get in his way.

The shadows were deep there under the trees, but the icy coating on the trees and bushes seemed to give off a faint glitter, reflecting back the light from the flashlights that Niki and Darwin were waving around. The flashlights pinpointed their positions as exactly as if they were caught on stage by spotlights. There was a glow all around them, as if the air was full of tiny particles of ice. The scene would have been breathtakingly pretty if it wasn't so breathtakingly cold, and she wasn't so damn scared.

Then she caught sight of Gabriel, easing up behind Darwin, every step as slow and careful as that of a big cat stalking an antelope. Lolly remained frozen to the spot, afraid to move, afraid she'd make a noise that would distract him.

Gabriel lifted his makeshift club like a baseball bat. He was still well back, out of the circle of light, but if either Darwin or Niki looked around they'd surely see him. The stance he took reminded her of watching him play baseball in high school, all those years ago when he'd been young and skinny and arrogant as all hell. He'd hit more than one home run in the old days; he looked poised to hit one now.

Lolly's heart pounded. She was tempted to cover her eyes with her hands, to hide from reality like a two-year-old playing hide-and-seek, but she had to watch. She had to know what was happening. If she was a betting woman she'd put everything she had on Gabriel. But nothing in life was certain, not even Gabriel McQueen, and tonight their lives hung in the balance.

Abruptly Niki screamed something and turned off her flashlight. Darwin wasn't as fast, and Gabriel stepped forward, swinging away, his muscular arms bringing the limb around so fast it made a whistling sound. Darwin dropped his flashlight and ducked. Instead of a solid blow, the limb glanced off his head, and with a growl like an animal, Darwin whirled and leapt on Gabriel.

Gabriel couldn't swing again because Darwin was inside his reach, so he shifted his hands apart on the limb and used it like a bar, making short, hard jabs with the ends and lightning-fast moves to block the wild punches Darwin was throwing, beating at Gabriel with the pistol. The flashlight Darwin had dropped had rolled to the side, pointing away from them, so they weren't much more than a massive shadow. Gabriel was taller, more muscular, but Darwin was still riding a meth high and was impervious to pain. He landed a solid kick behind Gabriel's knee and Gabriel went down, but he dragged Darwin with him.

Where was Niki? Lolly realized she could no longer see the woman and she looked around wildly, half-expecting Niki to leap out of the darkness at her, or rush to Darwin's defense, but . . . no Niki. Either she'd seized the opportunity to run, or she was biding her time, looking for an opening to either shoot Gabriel or bash him in the head. Lolly couldn't tell which of the rolling, cursing, grunting men on the ground was Gabriel and which was Darwin, so likely Niki couldn't either.

Abruptly Lolly realized that she was too far away to help Gabriel if Niki attacked. Without letting herself think about how likely she was to get hurt or killed for her efforts, she copied Gabriel and felt around on the ground until she found a stick of her own, a broken limb that had fallen recently enough that it hadn't rotted yet. It wasn't as hefty as Gabriel's limb, but it was better than nothing. No longer worried about remaining quiet, Lolly rushed toward the fight.

Where was Niki?

Lolly grabbed the fallen flashlight and frantically shone it around, trying to spot the woman. If she was there, she was hidden behind a tree or a bush. She could be behind them, to the left, the right, anywhere . . . even on the way back to the house. Lolly had seen only the two weapons, but that didn't mean there weren't more—belatedly she realized that the fact that Darwin was trying to hit Gabriel with the pistol instead of just shooting him meant that he'd fired all the bullets in the gun and didn't have any more, at least not with him.

Was Niki out of bullets, too? Was she running after more, or simply running? No way to tell. Lolly darted a quick glance at the fight. Darwin had torn Gabriel's knit cap off and was trying to head butt him in the face. Quick as lightning, she darted in and slapped Darwin in the face with her stick, which wasn't big enough to stop him but did briefly pull his attention to her. Gabriel seized that brief moment of inattention to punch Darwin in the face with his gloved fist. The sound was sickening, but Darwin didn't seem to even notice.

Gabriel was bigger, more muscular; he should have been able to take Darwin down in a matter of seconds, Lolly thought, then remembered how crazed meth could make people. She'd read reports of meth users who had been shot several times by the police and who not only didn't go down, but kept attacking. Darwin fought like a man possessed, sounds of maniacal rage growling in his throat like an animal.

She had never seen a real fight before, just the Hollywood staged version, never realized how much dirtier and noisier it was. This wasn't standing toe-to-toe and slugging it out, this was kicking and punching and gouging and anything else the two combatants could do to hurt each other. There were grunts and curses, the sickening thuds of gloved fists against flesh, the icy ground crunching beneath them. Their heavy winter coats prevented any significant damage to their bodies, prolonging the fight and increasing the odds that Darwin might land a lucky punch.

Maybe she could help. Lolly eased closer, raising her stick so she was ready to strike if the chance presented itself, but holding on to the flashlight handicapped her because she had only one free hand to hold the stick. She couldn't worry about Niki; the woman was either there or she wasn't. All she could do now, Lolly thought, was help Gabriel in any way she could.

The grappling men rolled almost out of the light, and when they stopped Darwin was on top. He drew back his hand and something was in it. Lolly didn't hesitate, didn't try to identify what he held; she simply leapt forward, swinging the stick with all her might, and began trying to beat the hell out of the man who'd tried to rape her. She dropped the flashlight, gripped the stick with both hands, and hit him again and again, on the head, the shoulders, anywhere she could reach.

With a howl he launched himself off Gabriel, straight for her. She staggered back, sick terror blooming in her stomach, her chest. Her feet went out from under her and she went down, Darwin on top of her and his hands fumbling for her throat. He began squeezing.

Then he was gone, lifted off her as if he were a child. Gabriel's expression was cold and fierce as he hammered his big right fist over and over into Darwin's face. Darwin was too stunned by the blows to fight back; he threw his arms across his face to protect himself and began sobbing. "Don't hurt me, man, don't hurt me," he pleaded. "I ain't done nothing to you, have I? Huh? What'd I do?"

Lolly struggled to a sitting position, staring at him in disbelief. He'd changed from enraged animal to pathetic loser in the space of a few seconds.

"Shut the fuck up," Gabriel snarled, breathing hard. He wrenched Darwin's arms behind his back, shoving them high, and looked around for something to secure them. "Get the laces from his boots," he said to Lolly.

She didn't want to get anywhere near Darwin, didn't want to touch him in any way, but she made herself half-crawl to where Gabriel held him, taking care to stay to the side so he couldn't kick her in the face. Gingerly she began picking at the leather lacings. They were wet and hard to handle, and she had to use both hands.

Gabriel's head swiveled as he looked around. He was still breathing hard and fast, and his expression . . . he was really pissed, to put it mildly. "Where did the other one go?" he asked Lolly. There was a savage note in his tone.

"I don't know," she replied. She was doing some hard breathing herself, and she paused a moment to take a few deep breaths. "She turned off her flashlight, and I guess she ran. I haven't seen her since then."

Gabriel turned his attention back to a weeping Darwin. He wrenched Darwin's arms harder and higher, putting agonizing strain on the shoulder sockets. "Do you have more ammo or weapons back at the house?"

"No," Darwin said, shaking his head. "I swear, we don't. Buddy, please, you're tearing my arms out of my shoulders!"

"I'm not your fucking buddy," Gabriel said. "And if you lie to me, I *will* tear your arms off and beat you to death with them, got it?"

"I'm not lying!" Darwin shrieked. Snot was running from both sides of his nose, dripping in his mouth. "Niki and me, we just have the two guns and what bullets are in them. That's usually enough. Ow! Ow! Stop, please stop!"

Usually enough. Lolly wondered how many other homes he and Niki had invaded, how many women he'd hurt, raped, murdered.

Deep in the forest, there was a sudden crack as sharp as a gunshot, followed by a crash and a thud. For a moment of sheer panic Lolly thought Darwin had been lying and Niki *did* have another weapon, but then she realized what had happened: limbs were beginning to give way under the weight of the ice.

"What the hell was that?" Darwin asked, a new fear in his quavering voice.

Neither Lolly nor Gabriel bothered to tell him what was happening.

"Now what?" she asked, looking up at Gabriel before returning her attention to Darwin's boot laces. They didn't know where Niki was; Darwin was unarmed, would shortly be secured, but it wasn't as if they could call the sheriff and have their prisoner collected and jailed within a matter of minutes. She didn't want to spend the night in the same house with him, not even if Gabriel hog-tied and gagged him, and she didn't think they could manage to get him down the mountain tonight. With limbs already beginning to come down, it was too dangerous to go anywhere tonight.

Gabriel opened his mouth to answer and Darwin suddenly threw himself backward in a convulsive movement that knocked Gabriel off balance, and wrenched his arms free from Gabriel's grasp.

With an inhuman roar he went for Lolly. Crouched

down the way she was, she didn't have a chance to run. He knocked her flat; she was hit with a force that knocked the breath out of her, and banged her head hard on the frozen earth. She heard a ripping sound as she slid across the rough, icy ground, then he was on her and trying for her throat again.

Gabriel recovered his balance and launched himself forward, both hands grabbing Darwin by his coat collar and slinging him off Lolly. Darwin surged to his feet, came at them again. Gabriel pivoted, planted his foot, and smashed his elbow backward into Darwin's face. There was a sickening crunch, and Darwin was suddenly boneless, his body oddly slack as he slumped to the ground. His eyes were open and staring, and twin black trickles of blood leaked from his nostrils.

Gabriel spared him only the briefest glance. "He's dead." His tone didn't reveal a shred of regret. The elbow to the nose, smashing it and driving bone fragments into the brain, hadn't been an accident.

Deep in the forest, another limb gave up its life with a sharp crack, and crashed down. Hard on the heels of it came another one, this one much closer.

Lolly was still on the ground, her eyes huge dark pools in a stark white face as she stared up at him. He leaned down and caught her arm, pulled her to her feet. "We have to go back to the house," he said. "We can't walk out now, not with limbs already coming down."

Solemnly she nodded, but she asked, "What about Niki? That's her name," she explained in a vague tone. She gestured at the body on the ground. "His name is Darwin. *Was* Darwin." A faint note of satisfaction leaked into her voice. Looking around, as if searching for the missing woman, she added, "She might be at the house."

"Maybe," Gabriel said grimly. "If she is, I'll handle it. From what this asshole said, they're out of ammo. If she didn't go back to the house, if she's out here somewhere . . . she can freeze to death, for all I care."

Still Lolly just stood there, and he gentled his tone. "Lolly, we don't have a choice." He bent and collected the flashlight Lolly had dropped, as well as Darwin's empty pistol. The pistol he slipped into his front pants pocket. His own flashlight was still secured in his coat pocket; he'd use the other one as long as the battery held out, because who knew how long they'd be in the house before the road was clear? If the electricity at the house hadn't already gone out, it would soon.

"I know," she said, her voice subdued.

God, he was cold. His knit cap was gone and the damn miserable rain had formed ice crystals in his hair. Not even his good cold weather gear could keep his body warm when he was losing so much heat through his uncovered head. He shivered convulsively, but forced himself to concentrate. He could see that Lolly's pants were dark with moisture from mid-thigh down, moisture that would leach all of her body heat away, too. They had to get dry. They had to get warm. The exertion of the fight had warmed him while it was happening, but now the letdown was leaving him even colder, and Lolly would be in worse shape because she had neither his muscle mass nor the experience in handling the aftermath of an adrenaline burn.

He turned her toward the house, his arm behind her back, urging her forward. "Are you cold?" he asked, though of course she was.

"I was," she said. She sounded exhausted. He'd expected that; it was normal. "I don't think I am now, though. But I can't feel my feet."

He shuddered again, his body trying to generate some heat, and suddenly he noticed that Lolly wasn't shivering. Shit, that wasn't good. She was hanging in there now, but he had to get her to the house in a hurry.

He left Darwin's body where it was; the only other option was to carry it out, and he had to devote what energy he had left to getting himself and Lolly out of these damn woods and back up the mountain to the house.

Cautiously they worked their way back to the pavement. They'd have to stay on the weedy edge where they'd have at least marginal footing, which meant they would be beneath the dangerous and increasingly ice-coated trees that leaned over the road, but they really had no choice because the road was the fastest way up. Whether they stayed in the woods or went by the road, they had to face the possibility of being crushed by a falling limb, so the less time they spent under the trees, the better. He kept his arm around Lolly, pushing himself as well as her. She didn't know how close to the edge he was skating, how much of an effort it was for him to walk, and he wanted to keep it that way. She'd been a trouper so far, but who knew where her breaking point was? He didn't think she'd give up, but now wasn't the time to find out.

He made his voice purposely steady and without emotion. "Earlier today, before I got to the house . . . did Darwin hurt you?"

He expected an immediate "No" that he wouldn't believe, or a painful "Yes" that would make him want to go back to the body and kill the man all over again, but Lolly hesitated before answering. "He tried. He almost—" Her voice broke and she stumbled.

Gabriel stopped, pulling her to a halt, and he turned the flashlight so he could see her expression. Her face was white and pinched with cold. The poncho had torn, and ice crystals had formed on her hair, just as they had on his. But her gaze was steadier now, even if her lips were blue. He cupped her face in the gloved hand that wasn't holding the flashlight. "He won't hurt you now."

Her answer was a nod, and in spite of the dire circumstances, it was relief that changed her expression. "Yeah, I know. You killed his ass." She paused, then added, "Thanks. Good job."

He almost laughed. Reassured, he started them walking again. She was going to be okay. Lollipop was turning out to be a pretty tough cookie. He continued to steady her as they walked up the hill, one slow, cautious step at a time. He stayed alert, watching and listening for the woman—Niki—but all he could hear was wind and the straining limbs of old, ice-covered trees.

Chapter Nine

Niki struggled to her feet. When that man had just appeared out of the darkness like a demon or something and attacked Darwin, her instinct for self-preservation had kicked in and she'd run like hell, without even a single thought about helping Darwin. She'd been looking over her shoulder instead of paying attention to where she was going, and she'd stepped in a shallow dip. Her feet had immediately gone out from under her, and she fell hard on her back, hard enough that she had lain there for a minute, too stunned to move.

When she'd been able to roll to a sitting position she'd just sat there on the frozen ground, watching Darwin and the man as they fought. She was out of bullets, so she couldn't do shit to help Darwin. The best thing she could do, she thought, was take care of number one; it wasn't as if Darwin would have been rushing to *her* aid, if the situation were reversed.

She couldn't see all that much, because of the trees and the way the flashlight had rolled when Darwin dropped it, but as she watched the fight she thought maybe Darwin would get hurt. The son of a bitch who'd rescued Lorelei was a big guy. She also thought that maybe Darwin would win the fight, because he was a lot stronger than he looked and he fought dirty. This was one of those wait-and-see situations, though she didn't want to wait too long. If things started looking bad for Darwin, she'd be better off taking care of herself. She had to get back to the house, get the ice they'd left on the coffee table . . . she needed some now, *right now.* It would make her feel a lot better, get rid of this crawling, antsy feeling.

But she must have knocked herself silly when she fell, because she was a little dizzy. It wouldn't be smart to head out too soon and fall again, really hurt herself. She'd sit there for another minute or so, see what happened to Darwin. Maybe she'd get to watch him kill the big dude.

So she sat very still, even though the ground was so cold the sensation went through her clothes like a sharp knife, even though her ass got wet, and she watched as Lorelei Helton came rushing out of the darkness, a stick raised high, and hit Darwin in the head with it. It didn't slow him down much, but it distracted him, and suddenly Niki knew this wasn't going to end well for Darwin. Two against one just wasn't fair.

Then Lorelei began beating at Darwin with the stick, over and over, *whap whap whap*. He'd had the big man down, but he let Lorelei get to him, and he rushed at her. Niki closed her eyes in disgust. Darwin never could plan worth a damn. That left the big man free, which was so damn stupid, and then of course the fight was over and Darwin was whining in that way that got on her nerves so bad. All she could do was shake her head. She couldn't help him, she had nothing except an empty pistol. Darwin was on his own in this, the stupid shit.

Her head felt better, the dizziness had subsided. Silently, while they were preoccupied with Darwin, she got to her feet and began easing away. The sound of renewed struggle made her stop and look again, and she saw the big man smash his elbow into Darwin's face, saw the way Darwin just sort of went down like an empty skin sack, and she knew he was dead. She'd seen enough dead people to recognize how they flopped, as if their bones had all of a sudden turned mushy.

She never had been able to depend on the dickhead, and now he'd gone and gotten himself killed.

Carefully, as silently as possible, she worked her way out of the woods. Twice there were really loud cracks and it scared the crap out of her until she figured out what had happened. Limbs were breaking off the damn trees. All around her, tree limbs were drooping under the weight of the ice; one of them could come down on her, at any time. This shit was creepy.

When she reached the road, she was so relieved to be out of those damn woods that she forgot about the ice and tried to run. Her feet immediately went out from under her and she went down hard on her knees. The pain was excruciating. Niki ground out a few cuss words as she slowly stood. She remained bent over for a moment, rubbing her knees, until she thought she could walk again. This time she eased to the shoulder—what there was of it—where she had better traction, and continued uphill at a much slower pace.

The cold, the darkness, the keening wind, the creepy ice . . . all of it surrounded her, and she realized how alone she was, how horribly alone, with no one to turn to. Darwin hadn't been much, but at least he'd been there. Now he was dead, because that big man was a murdering bastard. He was dead, she was alone, and she was outnumbered. On the up side, the Blazer belonged to her now. It wasn't as if Darwin would be needing it again.

As she walked, Niki got more and more pissed. If it hadn't been for that bitch Lorelei, Darwin might've won the fight, and instead of walking back to the house alone, she'd have Darwin beside her now. They'd get warm, do some meth to celebrate their victory, and maybe screw in Lorelei's bed.

Ice pelted her face, and she didn't like it. It was too fucking cold out here, and everything had gone wrong. Everything! They should've just robbed the grocery store this afternoon and gotten the hell out of town. Nothing had gone right from the minute she'd seen Miss Lorelei Bitch in her fancy Mercedes.

She caught a wisp of a voice on the wind and turned around to look down the long, winding driveway. Lorelei and the big guy were behind her, walking back to what they probably thought was safety. For a moment she saw a flash of light, and then it was gone. Like her, they were keeping to the side of the road and staying in the dark.

An idea came to her, and slowly she began to smile, even as a gust of stinging wind caught her full in the face. If things turned out right, when she left here she'd be driving that Mercedes instead of Darwin's piece-of-shit old Blazer, and those two would wish they'd never tangled with her . . . for a little while, anyway, then they'd never wish for anything again.

"As soon as we're around this curve, we should see the lights," Lolly said. Gabriel didn't know if she was encouraging him, or herself. Laboriously they plodded forward, rounded the curve, and she stopped as she searched the darkness for the beacon of the porch light that would encourage them to keep going, to reach the warmth and safety of the house.

There was nothing. The darkness was absolute. "The power's out," she said thinly.

"Yeah." Gabriel urged her forward, his arm literally

propelling her. He wasn't surprised by the loss of electricity, though he wished they'd at least made it back before the lines went down. Going toward a warm, brightly lit house was more of a psychological lift than seeing nothing but darkness at the end of the road. He needed something besides his own strength to keep them going, because he was fast running out of it.

Lolly was slowing down, her steps becoming heavier and more laborious; both of them had lost enough coordination that he was concerned. The cold was sapping her strength. She was about to give out, but he couldn't allow her to stop, not when they were so close to shelter. Shelter meant survival, and he couldn't afford to think of anything else.

He steadied Lolly, made sure they continued to move forward, and at the same time kept an eye out for Niki, who from all he could tell was no less deadly than her friend had been. Without a gun, would she even try to take him on? Experience with meth addicts said she would. She might try to get past him, get to Lolly. Even an empty pistol could kill, if you hit someone in the vulnerable temple area with it. Lolly was protected by all the stuff she'd tied over her head, but that was no guarantee she couldn't be hurt or killed.

Logically, Niki would realize she needed shelter just as much as they did. She might already be at the house, waiting for them. The electricity might not be off; she might have turned off the lights herself, so she'd have the advantage of surprise. He couldn't afford to assume she was either out in the cold, or inside the house; he had to expect anything, everything, and make no assumptions that could prove out wrong and catch him unprepared. Until Niki was accounted for, he couldn't let his guard down.

The night continued to be punctuated by the sharp retorts of limbs and trees snapping. The sound wasn't constant, but neither did it end. None of the trees closest to the road had fallen, not yet, but they would, and soon. For now the worst of the fall was deeper in the woods, where trees had been left untended for an eternity. At least the ones bordering the road had occasionally been trimmed.

"I don't suppose there's cut wood for the fireplace stacked by the back door," he said, trying to distract Lolly, trying to encourage her to imagine the comfort that waited ahead.

"No wood," she said, panting with the effort to keep going. He winced, kissing the dream of a fire good-bye, then she continued, "We converted to gas years ago."

Even better. "Hallelujah. Gas stove, too?"

"Yes."

"Water heater?"

"Uh-huh."

That was a relief, a huge one. They'd have some means of getting warm, and could spend the night in relative comfort. "Not much farther to go, Lolly, and we'll have a roof over our heads, heat, even some food."

"What if she's there?" Lolly asked, terror in her voice. Obviously her thoughts had been running along the same lines as his.

Gabriel shrugged. He was outwardly calm, inwardly concerned. "If Niki's there, I'll handle it. I promise."

She nodded in agreement, but didn't seem to be entirely convinced. Who could blame her? Their situation wasn't a good one, between the weather, the dark, and the nut-job who could come bursting without warning from out of the forest, or out of any closet or from under any bed.

Above them, a big engine abruptly roared to life.

Gabriel lifted his head at the sound. "Well, we know where Niki is," he murmured.

Lolly drew closer to him. "Yeah." She sounded nervous and wary.

Was Niki really stupid enough, or strung out enough, to try to drive down this hill? She wouldn't be starting the Blazer just to get warm, when all she had to do was go in the house. Why give her position away like that?

The sound of the engine changed, and gears shifted. Headlamps came to life, cutting through the darkness, catching in its beams the almost ethereal mist and making it glow.

———

Niki smiled. The Blazer was coated with ice and just getting the door open had been a bitch, but she'd managed it. She was alone, she was out of bullets, but Lorelei Helton and her big guy with his stick didn't stand a chance against her Blazer. She'd run them down like the dogs they were.

"For Darwin," she said, getting teary at the memory of the miles they'd covered in this Blazer. Maybe he hadn't been perfect; maybe he had cheated on her a few times. But through it all he'd been *hers,* and now he was gone. Darwin, gone. She couldn't believe it.

She gunned the engine and headed toward the hill and the center of the narrow drive. The rear end of the Blazer immediately started sliding around and she fought with the wheel for control, which she gained, and lost, and gained again. At least she was headed in the right direction. She was barely out of the yard when the headlights picked out her targets, there on the side of the road. The two murderers stood side by side, close together, stupidly looking up the hill, looking at her. They didn't realize what she had planned. They probably thought she was running away, that she was a coward who would give up and let them win, a coward who wouldn't make them pay for what they'd done.

Then the big guy seemed to realize what she planned to do, because he bodily lifted Lorelei and leapt into the tree line with her. A bloody haze of rage rose in Niki's vision. No fucking way was she going to miss them now, like a few trees could stop her.

They had to pay. They had to pay for killing Darwin; Lorelei had to pay for making a fool of her by going out a second-story window; she had to pay for leading Darwin on until he couldn't think about anything except getting in her pants. She'd catch them and ram them up against a tree, pinning their bodies there, and she'd laugh while they died in agony. She wanted that. She wanted it as much as she wanted her next hit. She'd have her hit soon, in just a few minutes, as soon as she'd taken care of this little chore.

The slope of the driveway increased, going down to the first sharp curve. Niki barely glanced at the pavement; her attention was on the spot where the big guy had gone into the woods. She spun the wheel to the left, and the entire Blazer began sliding sideways to the right. Swearing, she turned back to the right, trying to straighten the vehicle. The old Blazer responded, then the rear end swung around and damn if she wasn't sliding to the left now. Furiously she fought the vehicle. How in hell was she supposed to do what she wanted if the damn truck wouldn't go straight? What good was four-wheel drive if it didn't work on ice?

She jerked the wheel to the left, and both right wheels of the Blazer came off the ground. "Shit!" she yelped, suddenly realizing how close she was getting to the bottom, and the steep drop-off on the other side of the driveway. "*Shit!*" The Blazer settled back onto all four wheels; the big tires tried to grab traction but spun uselessly on the ice. The Blazer slid backward, then slowly began a sickening spin, around and around, gaining speed as it whirled toward the looming drop-off. She had the totally inane thought that it was almost like riding the teacups at Disneyland.

Niki screamed once, in rage and fear at the injustice of this stupid ice, then the Blazer's wheels lost contact with the ground and she plummeted over the side.

Lolly clung to Gabriel's wet coat, watching as the Blazer abruptly dropped out of sight. There was a brief moment of silence, then a horrible screech of metal being crushed and torn.

"Oh my God," she said in shock, then added, "Good!" She didn't think it made her a bad person that her first instinct was one of relief. Darwin was dead and Niki had just driven herself off the side of the mountain. For the first time in hours that had seemed as long as days, Lolly suddenly realized the terror was over. She was safe; cold to the bone, shivering, shaken in a way she hadn't known was possible . . . but safe.

"Stay here," Gabriel ordered, as he took a much larger flashlight from his coat pocket, turned it on, and stepped cautiously onto the road.

He had been her rock for the past couple of hours. Everything in her protested at being separated from him for even a few seconds, but she did as he instructed. There was no point in both of them going to look. Besides, she could barely walk, she was so cold. All she wanted was to sit down and close her eyes.

The sloping pavement was treacherous with ice. Gabriel slipped a couple of times, but both times managed to catch his balance and stay upright. Lolly breathed a sigh of relief as he reached the other side of the road and shone his light down the mountainside.

After a long moment, he made his way back across the driveway to Lolly. Turning off his powerful flashlight, he once more stowed it in his coat pocket and took out the much weaker flashlight Darwin had dropped. "The Blazer's about a hundred and fifty feet down. It met a tree head-on. The tree won. If Niki isn't dead she's seriously hurt, but I can't get down there to see." He frowned, because he didn't like not knowing for certain.

Lolly wouldn't have thought it was in her nature to be relieved at the news that someone, *anyone,* had died; it certainly wasn't like her to be willing to leave an injured woman in a wrecked car to freeze or bleed to death—or at least she hadn't thought it was like her. Darwin and Niki had changed her mind about several things. "Thank God," she whispered. She felt as if the world around her had warmed a little. Her fear of finding Niki waiting in the house, of the strung-out woman jumping out from behind a tree or springing out of a dark corner, was gone. She wanted to drop to the ground and sob in sheer relief, but she settled for a deep breath instead. It was too soon to declare victory, because she and Gabriel weren't home free. They still had to battle the ice, and the ice wouldn't make any stupid decisions, like trying to drive down a mountain in weather like this. The ice wouldn't do anything, other than exist, but its very existence reshaped the world.

"Come on," he said, "let's go get warm." He slid his arm around her, holding her upright as he propelled her forward. Without his aid, she couldn't have moved. The first few steps were an exercise in pain and lack of coordination; she could barely slide one foot in front of the other. She felt as if she had frozen to the spot, as if she could do nothing other than just stop. Gabriel was shivering violently against her; he was in better shape than she was, but that wasn't saying a lot.

"Do you need me to carry you?" Gabriel asked.

She was horrified at the idea. He could barely walk, and he thought he could *carry* her? "No, I'm fine," she said.

He made a gruff noise that made it clear he didn't think she was at all fine, but he didn't forcefully lift her and throw her over his shoulder.

In the total darkness, with only an increasingly weak flashlight beam lighting their way, they gingerly made their way across the icy yard. What had never seemed like much distance at all now seemed almost insurmountable, but they were barely shuffling along and every inch gained was paid for in agony. Finally she could very faintly make out the dark house looming just ahead of them, and only then did she really believe they could make it. "I'm sorry," she said softly, wondering if Gabriel would even hear her, with the wind howling as it was.

He glanced down at her. "Sorry for what?" he asked matter of factly as they negotiated the last few yards, maneuvering around her ice-coated Mercedes. The steps loomed like Mount Everest. She honestly wasn't certain she could go up them. "Sorry you got caught up in this mess. Sorry you had to kill a man. Sorry you're stuck here with me when I know you'd much rather be at your parents' house, with your son."

"You know about Sam?" he asked, surprised. His voice was breathless. Somehow he hadn't expected her to know anything about his life after he'd graduated from high school and joined the military.

"I've kept up with the news from here."

They reached the steps, and Gabriel gripped the railing with his left hand. His right arm tightened around her, and he physically hauled her up the steps, groaning in pain as he did. Then they were on the porch, but the howling wind was still blowing the rain in on them so there wasn't much improvement.

"I'm not sorry," he said, releasing her to bend over and catch his breath, gather his strength.

Without his support Lolly almost collapsed on the porch, but she wrapped one arm around a column and forced herself to remain upright. "I don't believe you." She even managed a credible snort.

"Seriously, Lollipop, do you think I'd be happy sitting in a nice warm house with my kid, eating soup and drinking coffee by the fire, when I could be up here freezing to death with you while we run from two crazy-ass meth addicts? Where's your sense of adventure?"

"I don't have one," she said, suddenly wheezing with laughter. She felt giddy, and she wasn't certain how much longer she could keep standing, but right now what he'd said was one of the most hilarious things she'd ever heard. "And do *not* call me Lollipop." If he'd forgotten anything at all about her, why couldn't it have been that horrid nickname?

"Lollipop," he promptly returned, just as he'd done in high school. He straightened, grunting with the effort, and said, "We're idiots to be standing out here. Let's go inside."

"Easier said than done," she said, and abruptly her legs gave way and she sat down hard on the ice-crusted porch.

"Don't you fucking give up on me now, Lollipop," he grunted as he lurched toward the door. "I didn't haul you all this way to let you freeze to death on the porch."

It scared her that the concept wasn't all that far-fetched. It would be so easy just to curl up on the porch and relax, but she knew if she did she'd never make it inside. Fear drove her to roll onto her hands and knees, but that was as far as she could get. No way could she stand up. Laboriously she began crawling toward the door. "You just get the door open, hero," she said, "and I'll make it the rest of the way."

There was a horrible, gunshot of a sound at the edge of the woods, and a sixty-foot-tall tree snapped at the base, the entire thing crashing to the ground with a force that seemed to rattle the entire world. They both went motionless for a brief second, then Gabriel turned back to fumble with the doorknob and Lolly resumed her slow, clumsy crawl.

She wouldn't have survived tonight if it hadn't been for Gabriel. She would already be dead, shot or frozen or crushed beneath an ice-covered tree. She would have died a violent death, her last few hours spent in terror and pain, her last thoughts that of a horrible man attempting to rape her, and maybe succeeding. And wouldn't you know it, as soon as the danger had passed, they'd started arguing. Some things never changed. The *feel* of their squabble had changed, though. She wasn't angry, wasn't upset. Arguing with Gabriel had a comfortable feel to it, almost like coming home.

Home. She really *was* home. All she had to do was get inside, and she'd be safe. She wasn't shivering anymore, hadn't for . . . how long now? She was a native Mainer, she knew that wasn't a good sign. She could still think, hadn't suffered any of the disorientation that came with severe hypothermia, so she thought she'd be all right. But then again, if her thinking was impaired, would she even realize it?

Gabriel tried to open the door, but his ice-coated

gloves couldn't grasp the doorknob. Swearing under his breath, he used his teeth to tug off the glove; the doorknob turned, and the door swung open to warmth and sanctuary. Turning back, he grasped Lolly's arm and half-dragged her over the threshold, far enough inside that he could shove the door closed. Then she fell over on her side on the floor and the strength left his legs and he fell beside her. He swore some more, struggling to his hands and knees, then he grabbed the newel post of the stairs and pulled himself to a mostly upright position. Lolly closed her eyes. She just wanted to lie here on the floor . . .

"Get up," Gabriel ordered, his voice commanding and harsh.

She cracked her eyelids open a little. "I don't want to get up."

"Too bad."

He clumsily swiped his hand over his head, and shards of ice flew from his hair. He shucked off the jacket and gloves, then leaned down and grabbed her arm again. She couldn't get her feet under her, so he dragged her to the first step of the stairs.

"I just need a minute—" Lolly began.

"You have to get dry and warm," he said, jerking at her first layer of clothes. He whipped off the ripped poncho and ice crystals flew, hitting the floor and a nearby table and instantly melting.

"Leave me alone," she said fretfully, slapping at his

hands. "We're inside now. Just let me rest for a little while."

"Not until you're warm." He continued to peel away clothes, and she let him. A part of her wanted to fight, just on principle, but she was so tired and moving was so difficult that fighting him was impossible. He pulled her to her feet and she closed her eyes and just stood there, swaying. It was wonderful to be out of the ice, out of the cold. She could sense the warmth around her, lingering heat from before the power had gone out, but she couldn't really feel it.

"Open your eyes, Lollipop," Gabriel barked.

With an effort she opened her eyes and scowled at him. "Why can't I just sleep?"

By the light of the flashlight he'd placed on the floor, pointed upward to reflect off the ceiling, she saw the worry on his face, the anger. "Not yet."

And suddenly she knew what he'd been doing, calling her Lollipop, all but picking a fight. He'd been trying to get her angry, keep her going.

Touched, feeling her insides turning to mush, she reached up and laid her cold hand along his rough cheek. "I'm sorry I snapped at you," she said.

"Did you snap? I didn't notice. You must be out of practice. Now stop apologizing and get out of those clothes," he ordered. "All of them."

Chapter Ten

Niki slowly lifted her head, not quite sure where she was or what had happened. She stared around her, trying to make sense of her surroundings, but the effort was too much and she closed her eyes, let her head rest against something cold and hard. She felt . . . she felt as if a giant had picked her up and thrown her down on the ground, as if her entire body had been stunned. Had she fallen out of bed? No, she wasn't in a bedroom, she was in . . . what was she in? She didn't know where she was. Nothing looked right.

Then, like a light switch being flipped, her memory clicked and it all came back in a rush. Darwin. The Helton woman and that big dude. The storm, the ice, and the edge of the world.

The dashboard lights glowed softly, even though

the engine was dead. One headlight shone, marking her spot in the night. All she could see through the shattered windshield was the tree that had stopped her descent down the mountainside. The entire front end of the Blazer was crumpled, the dash twisted and crushed and caved in on itself. Slowly she turned her head, because she felt as if it wasn't securely attached to her neck. What a weird feeling; she didn't like it. But her neck worked, and that was good.

A big limb had crashed through the window, impaling the passenger seat. Broken glass was strewn about the front seat, and cold wind whipped into the cab from all the broken windows.

Niki touched a hand to her head, felt the sticky blood there. Her entire scalp throbbed, and she was shaking from head to foot, one big convulsive shudder. She couldn't stop shaking, couldn't make her muscles stop quivering. Damn it, she could've been killed, she could be dead right now, like Darwin. And it was all their fault!

A part of her wanted to stay right where she was. She was so tired, so cold. Moving would take more energy than she had. After a few minutes, though, her survival instinct kicked in. Ordering her thoughts was difficult, but determinedly she set about getting them all lined up. She couldn't stay here. Once the battery wore down, she wouldn't have even the little bit of light she now had. She'd freeze to death here, in the dark and cold, if she didn't bleed to death first. Again she gingerly touched her head. The cut there was bleeding, but wasn't as bad as it could have been. Hell, she was alive, and she didn't seem to be missing any body pieces, so she'd already come out ahead. She listened, wondering if Lorelei and the big guy were working their way down the mountain looking for her, to come help . . . but there weren't any voices. There was wind, there was ice, and the creaking of the tree. That was it. Those bastards had left her here to die. What kind of people would do something like that?

She stared at the limb that had come through the windshield, imagined what would've happened if it had been just a foot or so to the left, and shuddered.

The driver's side window had broken out, too, and Niki turned her head in that direction as she attempted to orient herself. Most of the light from the one remaining headlight was blocked by something, maybe the bumper, but some leaked out to show her where she was.

On the side of a freakin' mountain, perched on an old, creaky, badly damaged tree that was coated with ice. If the tree went, if it snapped and gave way, the Blazer would go the rest of the way down. She doubted she'd be so lucky the next time some obstacle stopped what was left of the truck.

Niki pulled the door handle and pushed. When nothing happened she pushed again, putting all her weight, such as it was, into the task of opening the door. The Blazer creaked and rocked and she stopped for a moment. Anger flared up inside her, making her forget her physical pain. Everything that had happened so far—the storm, Darwin's death, the destruction of the Blazer, and Niki's injuries, even the fact that the damn door wouldn't open—it was all Lorelei Helton's fault. That bitch, look what she'd done. If she'd just stayed where she'd been told to stay, none of this would've happened.

Where was her flashlight? She felt around for it but couldn't find it, and she didn't have time to look for it. There was just enough light from the truck to show her the way. The door wasn't going to open, she finally decided, so she heaved herself up and crawled through the broken window, her movements cautious so as not to rock the Blazer. As she crawled out into the cold wind, she decided the vehicle was pretty firmly caught against the tree.

The slope was so steep she couldn't stand upright. Clinging to the wrecked truck, Niki looked down at herself. She hadn't escaped the wreck entirely unscathed. Her head was bleeding, there was a huge rip in the right thigh of her jeans and blood was seeping from it, and her shoulder hurt. It wasn't broken, but it might've been. Still, as she looked up to the top of the slope, she felt pretty damn lucky, and she knew there had to be a reason for her survival.

She had survived so she could take revenge on those who'd done her and Darwin wrong.

She had survived so she could do what was right.

With ice covering everything, the only way up the steep hill before her was to crawl, so that's what she did. With every inch she moved forward, she was more and more certain of her purpose. She wasn't going to run. She wasn't going to find a warm spot and cower until morning. She was going to kill Lorelei Helton and the man who murdered Darwin. After all, it was justice, plain and simple.

"How many damn clothes do you have on?" Gabriel growled, pulling at yet another shirt.

"Enough!" she said, slapping at his hands. "Stop that! I can get my own clothes off."

"Then do it." He couldn't carry her, but he could bully her and half-drag her and push her up the stairs, with only the bobbing light from one increasingly dim flashlight to show him the way. In a newer house maybe there would be a full bath downstairs, but the only downstairs bathroom in the Helton house was a half bath that had been added on years earlier.

A hot shower would warm Lolly up. Shower, dry clothes, warm food. It was a simple plan, a necessary plan, if she'd just cooperate.

"I can walk, you know," she said, sounding grumpy but also more tired than he was comfortable with. He didn't think she was so far gone that she needed hospitalization—not that he could've gotten her to a hospital if she did—but she was on the edge. Another half hour outside, and a hot shower wouldn't have been such a great idea.

"Yeah, sure. If you can walk, then do it. You need to get in the shower as fast as you can."

"All right, all right." She began struggling up the stairs, so he didn't have to do all the work. "When I'm warm," she added with a sigh, "I'm going to wrap myself in the comforter and sleep for days." She stopped abruptly. "Wait. Did you lock the front door?"

"Yes." He had, out of sheer reflex. On the very slim chance that Niki had survived the crash and somehow managed to make it back to the house, a locked door wasn't a bad idea. It was unlikely that anyone could've been mobile after a crash like that one, but stranger things had happened. Why was it a drunk always walked away from a bad accident, leaving his victims dead while he shook his head and wondered what had happened? It was much the same for people strung out on drugs; he'd seen it many times over the years. God watched over fools and drunks, he'd heard. Didn't make much sense to him, but some days it proved to be true.

"Bathroom?" he asked as he reached the top of the stairs.

"This way." Lolly pointed, and he followed her lead to a door that opened onto a long, narrow bathroom that contained both a tub—standard issue, not a whirlpool—and a separate shower. These days it would be considered crowded and on the small side, but for its time this bath was quite a luxury. Gabriel didn't care how small or large the room was, he only

cared that there was a shower and plenty of hot water—
as well as, hallelujah, a radiant gas heater built into
the wall. He couldn't think of many things that would
be more welcome right now than that heater.

"We're going to get you warm," he said as he closed
the toilet lid and sat Lolly on it. He placed the flashlight on the back of the toilet tank, standing it up so
the light would reflect off the white ceiling. He
reached into the shower to turn on the water and let
it get warm. He just hoped he didn't get the temperature too hot, because even though he'd been wearing
gloves his hands were so cold he couldn't really judge
how warm the water was.

He turned around and saw that Lolly had closed
her eyes again. "Wake up!" he snapped. "Lolly! Get
your clothes off!"

She jumped like a startled deer, her eyes popping
open. "Jeez," she muttered. "All right. All I did was
close my eyes for a second."

"You can close them later, after you're warm." As
she struggled out of her clothes he turned and lit the
gas heater, turned it on as high as it would go, then
held his hands before the flames to soak up the heat.
Ah, God, that felt so good it hurt. He held them there
for just a minute before turning his efforts to stripping out of his own clothes. "Stripping" was the wrong
word, because it implied speed. He struggled out of
them, just as Lolly was doing. The fabric was cold and
uncooperative, his hands were cold and uncooperative, and his jeans were cold, uncooperative, *and* wet,

which greatly upped the uncooperative factor. He could barely keep his balance, and finally he propped himself against the sink so he could finish. He'd have liked to sit down and close his eyes, too, but he was afraid if he did he wouldn't be able to start moving again.

He half-expected Lolly to protest but she didn't, either at taking her clothes off in front of him or him getting naked, too. He was trying to keep her alive and stay alive himself, and she was either practical enough to shove other concerns to the side, or she knew how close she was to being in real trouble. She was also human enough to dart a quick, troubled glance at his genitals.

"Don't worry," he reassured her in a growl. "It's drawn up so far I couldn't find it with both hands and a flashlight."

"Then I hope you don't need to pee any time soon," she retorted, and if he hadn't been so cold he would have laughed at that. As it was, he couldn't even manage a smile.

Before they got in the shower he checked out her fingers, stooped to look at her toes. They were blue with cold, but didn't yet show any signs of the white that signaled frostbite. Then he pulled her from her seat on the toilet, clamped his arm around her waist again, and hauled her into the shower.

Lolly whimpered as the warm water sluiced over her. He couldn't tell if the whimper was from pain or pleasure; she was so cold, either was possible.

Thank God the showerhead was set high on the wall, so he could get completely under the spray. He stepped under it, letting the water beat down on his head and melt the ice that crusted his hair. The water hit his cold skin like pellets; it was both pleasure and pain, and he all but whimpered, too.

"You're hogging the water," Lolly complained, and he solved that problem by wrapping his arms around her and pulling her against him, so the warm shower rained down on both of them. With a shuddering little sigh, Lolly put her arms around his waist, nestled her head on his chest, and closed her eyes again.

Now that they were actually in the shower, closing their eyes seemed like a damn good idea, so he propped his chin on top of her head and let his own eyelids drift down.

"God, this feels so good," she whispered.

He wasn't sure if she was talking about the heat or him, and he sure as hell wasn't going to ask. He didn't care. He could feel the cold leaving him, draining away under the driving water pressure. He could feel his head warming, feel the pain receding.

A part of his brain—a dangerously small part— remained on alert, listening for anything he might hear over the sound of the shower. He hadn't been able to go down the mountain and make certain Niki was dead, and as long as that uncertainty remained he couldn't completely relax. He and Lolly were vulnerable here in the shower, but they had to get warm, and when he weighed the two factors against each other getting warm trumped everything else. He'd been so cold he was almost beyond functioning, beyond helping either Lolly or himself, and if Niki had come at them again he wasn't certain he could have managed much in the way of a reaction.

Two things weighed in their favor. One, even if Niki was still alive he saw no way she wouldn't be injured, probably too severely to be able to move. Two, if by some perverse miracle she *was* able to move, she had to be as cold as they were—unless she'd been using meth for so long she'd gone into hyperthermia, which would be doubly dangerous in this weather because she wouldn't feel the cold, wouldn't properly protect herself from it.

When he was recovered and dry, he'd bundle up and go back outside, check out the crash scene again. From a different angle he might be able to see if Niki was still in the mangled Blazer. Until then, all he could do was handle one problem at a time and stay alert for any strange sounds.

Then another problem presented itself.

As he'd gotten warmer he'd become aware of how good Lolly felt pressed against him, soft and shapely, with very nice curves that had been hidden beneath all those layers of clothes she'd been wearing. The spray of water hit her and ran down perfect, smooth flesh. She was wet and soft and naked . . .

Gabriel ran his hands up and down Lolly's back, trying to create heat with friction as well as with the hot water. He could feel the change in her as she warmed; she relaxed, her breathing became more normal and her stance became stronger, steadier. She was going to be okay. They'd made it, survived a hellish situation, and for the first time in hours he let himself relax from a state of high alert.

He almost went to sleep there, standing in the hot shower with Lolly wrapped in his arms. Maybe he did doze, for just a second. Maybe she did, too, because other than the rise and fall of her chest she didn't move.

Gradually he surfaced from that almost-sleep. The ice storm continued its deadly accumulation outside, but he and Lolly were safe inside, warm, protected, free to simply feel and react. As his body absorbed the heat of the water he felt as if he, too, were melting, until there was nothing left in the world but his body and hers.

It was easy to stand beneath the spray and hold on to Gabriel and let everything else go. No more fear, no more cold. Just this.

Gradually she became aware that he no longer had any problem finding his penis. It swelled between them, long and thick and rock hard. Vaguely startled—Gabriel McQueen was turned on by *her*?—and yet completely accepting, Lolly opened her eyes and looked up to find him staring down at her with the set, intent expression of a man who wanted sex and knew he was about to get it. Even in the dim, fading light of the flashlight, she could see the glitter in his eyes.

He smoothed her wet hair back from her face, cupped her bruised cheek with one big hand, then his mouth was on hers.

His hand was gentle. His mouth wasn't. He kissed like a marauder, hungry and fierce, demanding and taking surrender. Without thought or hesitation she gave him what he wanted. Nothing mattered beyond this moment, beyond the sudden reckless fever that flared to life between them. They could both be dead, so easily. They weren't; they were here, alive, warm, and they came together in a frenzy.

He lifted her, crushed her against the tiled wall under the showerhead so the water continued to beat down on them. Instinctively she wound her legs around his hips, the position opening her to him. Reaching down, he positioned his penis; the thick head brushed against her soft flesh, barely entered, and that was enough to make her whimper in need. She writhed, searching for more, and he gave it to her. With a groan he pushed deep, stealing her breath, both easing and increasing the sharp need. She groaned, too, at the taking of him, at the sensation of being stretched by the heavy fullness already pumping back and forth inside her. Lolly closed her eyes and tightened the grip of her legs around him, riding out the storm.

She came hard and fast, crying out, trembling and arching under the onslaught of sheer pleasure. He gripped her ass and moved her back and forth on him, short, fast strokes that intensified her orgasm and was almost too much to bear. Moaning, she dug her fingernails into his shoulders as the sensation peaked, subsided, then abruptly peaked again. She couldn't bear it, couldn't stand any more, and tears suddenly flooded her eyes. "Please," she said, and with a shudder and a deep groan he buried himself to the hilt and came, too, pumping hard and fast and gradually changing his rhythm to slow and rolling as he drew out his own pleasure.

In the aftermath there was silence, but a silence in which they clung together, gulping in air and trying to regain some strength in legs that had none. His heavy weight crushed her into the wall; if it hadn't been for the support of that wall, she suspected they would be on the floor of the shower. Her arms were wound around him, and absently she stroked the back of his neck, absorbing the feel of him naked against her. He was all hard muscle, every inch of him, and everything in her that was woman delighted in being pinned there with his penis still heavy inside her.

He roused up enough to reach out and turn off the shower with a snap of his wrist. The water was cooling anyway, and the efficient gas heater had already warmed the bathroom to pleasantly toasty.

Neither of them said anything. There would be a time for talking, but that time wasn't now. For now, they just *were*, adrift in the moment.

Gently he cupped one breast with his big, hard hand. His rough thumb brushed back and forth over her nipple and she felt that touch everywhere, tingling along nerve endings that hadn't yet quieted. She pressed her lips to his wet shoulder, then with a soft sigh let her head rest there.

Her thoughts drifted as relaxation spread through her bones. She loved this house, she thought drowsily, always had: the smells, the large rooms, the old furniture. Until tonight, all her memories in this place had been good ones. She didn't want her last memory made in this house to have anything to do with Darwin and Niki. When she walked away, when she said good-bye, she wanted her final memories to be good ones. Gabriel had given her that, replaced horror with pleasure, bad with good.

Lolly moved her mouth, tasted the wet skin of his neck and inhaled his heat. His breathing changed; his body shifted, but not away from her. He moved closer, deeper into her, and nothing had ever felt so right.

"How do you feel?" he asked, his voice gruff and steady and soothing.

"Better." She was wonderfully warm, wonderfully lethargic. They did need to get dried and dressed, but not just yet. She kissed his neck again. "You?"

"Yeah. Better." He paused. "Uh—Lollipop . . ."

She smiled, hidden against his shoulder. "I'm on to you, now. You're just trying to make me mad, calling me that," she said without heat.

"Well, yeah. That was always the point," he said, as if that were obvious.

"I had a terrible crush on you." She would never have admitted that before, she would have been mortified if he'd ever suspected . . . and now it didn't matter.

He pulled his head back a little, looking down at her. "No shit?" He sounded pleased. "You didn't act like it."

"Of course not. I was a teenage girl. I'd have died rather than let you know." Thank God those years were behind her; no way would she ever want to relive the angst and raging hormones, the excruciating insecurity.

"I liked fighting with you," he admitted, his own mouth quirking in a little smile. "It got me going."

Men, she thought. They couldn't be the same species. She sighed, so content she could barely move. In that moment, everything was all right; with Gabriel inside her, with the flush of pleasure still fresh, she was content.

He stirred, reluctantly separating their bodies, and she let him. Her legs unlocked from around him, her thighs sliding down his until her feet once more touched the floor. He tilted her chin up so their eyes met. "Are you on the pill?" His voice rumbled in his chest, deep and gruff.

She couldn't help smiling. "It's a little late for that question, isn't it? But the answer is, yes, I am."

"That's good." He rubbed his thumb over her lower lip. "We can do this again."

"Right now?" she asked, startled, and he laughed.

"Fifteen years ago, yeah, but now it'll take me a couple of hours to recover. Come on, let's get dry."

Her legs weren't quite steady, but she felt much better, almost normal. She felt a bit self-conscious at being naked in front of him, which was a little silly at this point, but her cheeks heated as she stepped out of the shower and quickly headed for the linen closet, where she grabbed two towels. She tossed one to him and briskly began drying herself, standing close by the wall heater.

"I have a few cans of soup in the kitchen," she said, trying to sound as normal as possible.

"Sounds good to me." Gabriel scrubbed the towel over his hair, then paused to glance at the cold, wet clothes on the floor. "I don't suppose your dad left any clothes behind."

"No," she said. "They cleared all their personal items out a couple of years ago." Then she laughed. "He's six inches shorter than you, and his waist is probably ten inches thicker. I don't think any of his clothes would have fit you, anyway. We'll hang your clothes in front of one of the fireplaces; they should be dry by morning."

"Great." His voice rumbled. "Guess I'll be bare-assed naked until then."

"I don't mind," she said, and smiled at him. "But we

have blankets, several wall heaters, a couple of gas fireplaces, plenty of candles, and those cans of soup I told you about. I have some instant coffee, too."

His eyes lit at the mention of coffee, even instant coffee. "That'll do."

"I'm starving," Lolly said, realizing as she spoke how true those words were. She also realized that she wouldn't mind if she and Gabriel were stuck here for a few days. After what had just happened in the shower, so quickly and naturally that she'd barely had time to think, she didn't wonder at all how they'd pass the time.

Life took some astonishing turns, she thought. She never could have anticipated this, never thought she'd be so comfortable with him, or that making love with him, of all people, would feel so right.

Good Lord. *Gabriel McQueen.*

Chapter Eleven

Niki huddled on the floor in a dark corner of the kitchen, listening to the water running upstairs as she tried to force herself to throw off the chill. She strained to hear more. It wasn't certain that Lorelei and the big guy would be together, though it was likely. One of them might be in the living room, in another room upstairs . . . right around the corner.

Did they know she was here? Had they heard her?

In their earlier exploration of the house, before everything had gone to shit, Darwin had checked out the mud room and the back porch for portable stuff they could pawn, when the money they got from the Helton woman ran low. He hadn't found shit, naturally, but at the moment that didn't matter. What mattered, what she'd counted on as she'd crawled up an icy slope and made feverish plans for the night, was that he hadn't bothered to relock the door when he'd come back in. She'd entered the dark house through the back door, into the mud room, into the kitchen, cold and shaking and hurting all over. She'd felt her way to this corner, cowering and listening. That's when she'd first heard the water running and realized that at least one of them was upstairs.

The water stopped, and a moment later she heard faint voices, two of them. She couldn't tell what they were saying, but those voices assured her that no one was waiting around the corner; they were both upstairs. Relief washed through her; she could breathe again. She could think.

There wasn't much of anything in the house that could be used as a weapon, now that all the ammunition was gone, but what better place to find a weapon than the kitchen? Niki forced herself to stand, pushing past her pain and the lingering chill. Her hands were so cold, her entire body was so cold she could barely move. Now that she was inside that iciness would fade, but it wasn't happening fast. Once she had the place to herself she'd light a fire, kick back, take a hit, and relax. She'd earned it tonight.

Slowly she opened a drawer, then another, cautiously feeling around and not bothering to close them since that might make too much noise and she wasn't yet ready to face her enemies. She couldn't see much, but her eyes had adjusted to the dark and there was a touch of light, reflecting off the ice, coming through the kitchen window. There was just enough for her to see shadows and shapes as she felt around inside the drawers, finding nothing suitable. There was only the bare minimum in the way of utensils. After searching four drawers, she silently huffed in frustration, then she scanned the countertop and smiled at the dark shape she saw there.

A touch confirmed that the dark shape was a butcher block of knives. She grabbed the handle of the largest knife, and was horrified to find that her hands were so cold she couldn't properly grip it. What good was a knife if she couldn't hold it? She carefully placed the knife on the counter within easy rich, then removed her gloves and rubbed her hands together, bringing blood flow and warmth back. She would have liked to turn on the faucet and run warm water over her hands, but the sound of running water would alert the two upstairs, just as it had alerted her, so she didn't dare. She had to make do. After rubbing her hands for a minute she stuck them under her arms to absorb what body heat she had left.

With the return of warmth came a rush of pain. She was hurt, she didn't know how bad, but she thought about Darwin and how those two jerks had killed him, and she pushed the pain away. She'd deal with that later, after they were dead. The big dude would go first, because he was the most dangerous. He'd killed Darwin with his fucking *elbow*. One quick pop and that was it, no more Darwin. Lorelei was nothing. Niki knew she could take her with no problem, after the big dude was out of the way.

When she picked up the knife again, she was pleased with her grip. She could hold it properly now. She concentrated on listening again. For a moment there was nothing, then a board overhead creaked. There was a footstep, then another.

At first she'd been pissed because the power was out, but now she thought that would work in her favor. There were shadows and dark corners where she could hide, where she could wait and catch them by surprise. She had an advantage, a big one. She knew where they were; they thought she was helpless, dead, out of their lives.

They were wrong. She was like a ghost, a very dangerous ghost who intended to make sure they were both dead before the light of day gave them a chance to find her.

She remembered seeing a few candles and a couple more flashlights lying around, but searching for them would make too much noise, and any light she made would give her position away. That could wait. They'd know she was here soon enough, but not yet.

She was a part of the night, she thought, at once giddy and yet strangely detached, as if a part of her was floating along unconnected to her body. She was a shadow. She was death. With the knife gripped in her hand she listened, then took a few careful steps forward. She didn't need to see.

And they would never see her coming.

God, he hated pulling on his wet jeans, but Gabriel fought his way into them anyway. They'd started to dry, thanks to the gas heater in the bathroom, but were still unpleasantly damp and clammy. After everything he'd been through tonight, he could handle unpleasant for a while. Besides, once they got downstairs and started the fireplace, the jeans wouldn't be damp for long. His coat had kept his shirt dry, and his boots had protected his feet. Once the fireplace had the living room warmer, he'd strip off the jeans and drape them over a chair or something, shoved close to the fireplace so they'd dry faster.

Lolly had some clothes in her bedroom, which surprised him because she'd been wearing so damn many he thought for sure she'd had them all on. Her bedroom door, however, was locked from the inside. He'd be able to pop the lock with no problem, with a straight pin or a paper clip, neither of which he happened to have on him.

"There are both downstairs," she replied, when he said as much. She could have put her own wet clothes back on, as he had, but she couldn't stand the thought and instead got a thin blanket from the linen closet and wrapped it around her. "I'll wait until you can get my bedroom door open."

That suited him, he thought. Yeah, it was a real hardship, spending the night with a woman wearing nothing but a blanket, when he remembered *exactly* what she looked like and felt like underneath the cloth.

He hadn't intended to have sex with Lolly in the shower, but he sure as hell couldn't say he was sorry. He'd be lying if he said he hadn't wanted it, that he regretted what had happened. Whether or not it happened again . . . shit, if she touched him and smiled, if she put her mouth on him again, he likely wouldn't have any more control than he'd had the first time around.

It occurred to him that he didn't know if she was married or ever had been, if she had a husband or a boyfriend back home. Knowing Lolly, he suspected not. She wasn't the kind of woman who'd screw around on a man.

Then again, could he really say he knew her? People changed in fifteen years. Sometimes they changed a lot. And yet he felt as if he knew her, felt as if the fifteen years were maybe fifteen months instead, that the interval had given him time to see her in a different light and appreciate the differences. Maturity was a wonderful thing.

"You know," he said, as casually as he could manage, "we're probably going to have to walk out of here."

Lolly hugged the blanket closer and grimaced. "You're kidding me, right?"

"How much food and propane do you have handy?"

She sighed. "Enough for a couple of days, max."

"That's what I figured. We'll get warm, eat, sleep, wait for the sun to come up and listen for the tree fall to ease up a bit. By tomorrow afternoon, at the latest, the road crews should be out working. The road up the mountain is low priority, probably at the bottom of the list, but if we can make it down the hill we'll probably meet up with someone long before we reach town."

"And if we don't?"

He smiled at her. "Then we'll walk the rest of the way to town." After tonight, a long, difficult walk in the cold seemed like a cakewalk.

"I need something hot to eat before I even think about walking out of here." Bundled up in her blanket, Lolly headed into the hallway, and toward the stairs.

Lolly hated, hated, *hated* to go back into the kitchen. Because she hated it so much, she forced herself to keep going, to not hesitate. The memory of what had happened here remained too strong, even though so many other memories—good and bad—had been made tonight. But she wanted and needed warm food in her belly, and she refused to allow a dead man to keep her from it. He was dead; she wasn't. She'd won.

With the power out the electronic ignition on the stove wouldn't work, so she found the matches and lit a burner on the stove; the flame gave off heat and a little bit of light, enough for her to look for some candles and the oil lamps she knew were still here, some-where. She turned, and stopped dead in her tracks, hugging the blanket closer to her. Several drawers were standing open, and her heart lurched at the sight.

She took a deep breath and slowly let it out. Darwin and Niki must have been looking for something, but what? Anything that could be sold, she imagined. She wondered if she'd ever again be not afraid. From here on out was she going to jump at the sound of every ring of the doorbell or creak of the house? Would she be suspicious of every stranger?

Gabriel was in the living room, lighting the gas fire-place, laying their clothes out to dry. She wouldn't think about Darwin; she'd think about Gabriel. She would concentrate on finding the candles, getting some soup heated, then they'd settle down in front of the fire.

It hadn't bothered her before, but she suddenly realized how lumpy she'd looked in all those clothes, layer upon layer. How mortifying, no matter how nec-essary it had been. She wanted to look good for Gabriel, and wasn't that a kick in the pants? She'd never cared very much what anyone thought of her appearance, much less Gabriel, but now . . . now she wished she had the blue sweater that her friends said made her eyes shine, and those really expensive snug jeans that made her butt look fantastic. She touched her wet hair. She could really use a hair dryer, too.

With one hand holding the blanket, which was

wrapped tightly around her, Lolly collected a sauce pan from the cabinet, then grabbed a can of soup from the pantry. She set the can on the counter, reached into an open drawer for the can opener . . . and froze.

When she'd last been in this kitchen, she'd been trying to fight off Darwin, and she had instinctively scanned the room for weapons. At that time, the block of knives had been full—out of reach, but full. Now, the largest knife in the collection was gone.

Why would they have taken a knife when they both had guns?

A chill ran up her spine. Niki could've survived the crash and come back. They hadn't heard her breaking through a window, and Gabriel had locked the front door. But her keys had been in her purse, and Niki had had the purse.

Lolly could barely breathe. She'd been so intent on getting warm, so sure Niki was either dead or down for the count, she hadn't even thought about the keys.

The nightmare came roaring back. The fear and the cold gripped her.

"Gabriel!" she screamed, whirling to run, and she came face-to-face with the nightmare.

Niki—bleeding, limping, holding the missing knife in her raised hand—lurched toward Lolly.

Lolly threw herself backward until she slammed into the cabinet, and then she had no place to go. She grabbed the can of soup and threw it; it bounced off

Niki's shoulder. "Fuck!" Niki said furiously. "That hurt, bitch!"

Lolly grabbed the saucepan and threw it, and when Niki ducked she seized the chance to dart to the side, away from the cabinets. There was a small dried floral arrangement on the kitchen table; she threw that, too. Niki ducked again, and kept coming.

Then Gabriel was there, fast and silent on his bare feet, looming out of the darkness. He hit Niki from behind, the impact sending her crashing into the cabinets. She screamed with pain, tumbled to the floor. Gabriel pounced, grabbed the hand that held the knife, and slammed it against the floor over and over again until she lost her grip and the knife clattered to the floor.

Immediately, Niki began to wail. "Stop! I'm hurt! My arm . . . I think my arm is broken." She began to sob. "What was I supposed to do? You killed Darwin and then you left me out in the cold to *die*. How could you?"

Easy, thought Lolly. She didn't feel sorry for the woman at all, even though dried blood caked her face, her clothes. But Niki continued to whine; just like Darwin, she went from enraged attacker to pathetic beggar in a heartbeat. How many times had that act worked for them? Gabriel didn't buy it, though, and neither did Lolly.

"Shut up," he said brusquely, and reached for her other wrist to secure it.

Infuriated that her tactic hadn't worked, Niki

screamed and swung the empty pistol that she'd pulled from her coat. Gabriel jerked his head back but the barrel caught him on the outside corner of his right eye and whipped his head around. She surged up, shoving him back, and the blow had stunned him enough that for a second he couldn't react fast enough. Niki scrambled up and away, scooping up the fallen knife and lunging for the back door.

Gabriel gave a quick shake of his head and launched himself in pursuit.

Her heart beating so hard she could barely breathe, Lolly jerked open the cabinet door under the sink, grabbed the hammer from the small open toolbox that had been there as long as she could remember, and followed them both.

Chapter Twelve

Gabriel caught up with Niki on the back porch. The cold seared his bare skin. He had on nothing but a pair of wet jeans, not even a shirt he could pull off and use to snag the knife away from her. She whirled, lashing out with the knife, and he leapt back. She was nothing but a shadow in the darkness; only instinct, and experience gained by fighting with men who had been trained for combat, helped him avoid the blade. She was drug-crazed, unpredictable, and lethal as hell.

He wished he'd had time to grab something, anything, he could use as a weapon, or to block the slashing knife, but when Lolly had screamed his name he'd reacted instantly, without pausing to look around. He'd known, known without doubt, that somehow the homicidal bitch had not only survived the slide off the side of the mountain, but had managed to get out and make it back to the house. All he'd thought about was getting to Lolly before Niki could.

Niki darted in, slashed at him, darted back. She missed, but not by much. She came at him again, and he saw the glint of the blade swiping at his stomach. He jerked back, grabbed for her arm, missed. From the corner of his eye he saw more movement at the door, and his heart almost stopped. Lolly!

"No!" he yelled. The last thing he wanted was her out here in the dark, where he wouldn't be able to tell her from Niki, but Niki would know exactly who Lolly was. Niki whirled toward the new threat and he heard her laugh as she surged forward. He knew he couldn't get to her in time to grab her arm, knew he couldn't move fast enough to knock Lolly out of the way, but he tried anyway, leaping for her even as his heart whispered that he was too late, too late . . .

Lolly swung the hammer. She could barely make out a dark shadow coming toward her, but Gabriel yelled from somewhere to the left and she knew it wasn't him. It was so dark she had no real way to judge distance, but she swung as hard as she could and was almost astonished when the hammer struck something with a sickening sound that was both a solid thunk and yet somehow squishy.

Then Gabriel was there, enveloping her in a body-slam of a rush that knocked her back into the mud room. She knew it was him, knew his scent, felt the bareness of his arms and chest. They crashed to the floor and the impact knocked the hammer free from her grip. He rolled off immediately, leaping to his feet and whirling to meet Niki's next attack, but . . . nothing happened. No drugged-out maniac came through the door. There was nothing but silence from the back porch.

"Get my flashlight," Gabriel said, breathing hard, and Lolly scrambled to her feet. The blanket . . . somehow she'd lost the blanket and she was completely naked, but she'd worry about that later. Frigid air swept through the open door, stinging her flesh as she raced to the stairs where Gabriel had dropped his coat when they first came in. The fireplace in the living room was lit, providing enough light that she found the coat with no problem, fumbled in the pocket, pulled out the big foot-long flashlight, turned it on, then ran out to the back porch again.

Gabriel took the flashlight from her and shone it on the heap that lay on the floor. Niki was collapsed on her stomach, breathing shallowly, her face turned away from them. The knife lay on the floor beside her hand. Gabriel moved forward, kicked the knife well out of her reach, and only then did he stoop to pick it up. The beam of the flashlight plainly showed the damage the hammer had done to her head.

And even as they watched, she tried to heave herself to her knees. What was she, the fucking Terminator?

"Why won't she die?" Lolly whispered, evidently thinking along the same lines. "What do we have to do, put her in a vat of molten steel?"

And then Niki died, after all, very quietly. The shallow breathing stopped.

Gabriel caught Lolly's arm, steered her back into the house. Bending down, he snapped up the blanket and wrapped it around her. She was trembling like a leaf, and though there was a lot he needed to do, at the moment holding Lolly was more important than anything else on that list. "Are you okay?"

"Peachy," she whispered.

"Seriously, look at me."

She looked up at him, and what he saw assured him that she was indeed okay, or at least as much as someone unaccustomed to violence could be in such a situation. She wasn't happy, but neither was she collapsing under a ton of misplaced guilt. She'd done what she had to do, and she accepted that.

He kissed her, then left her standing in the middle of the kitchen hugging the blanket to her shivering body, and went back out on the porch. He crouched beside Niki, reached out and touched her throat in search of a pulse. Nothing. He blew out a sigh of relief.

Some of the freezing rain blew onto the porch, settling on Niki's body and on his bare skin. His feet felt almost as frozen as they had been an hour ago. He wasn't dressed for this shit, so he left Niki where she was, and went back into the house.

When he closed the back door he took a moment to lock it. Couldn't hurt.

The seconds dragged on, and Lolly listened hard. She should move, do something, follow Gabriel or run away. She found she could do nothing but stand there, hold tightly on to the blanket, and listen to her own heartbeat as she waited. Was it over? Was Niki going to somehow get up again, ignoring death? Lolly wanted peace; she wanted this night to be over.

She heard the back door close, and her heart matched its thud. A moment later Gabriel walked into the kitchen, blessedly alone and unharmed.

"Is it really over?" Her voice shook.

"It's over. She's dead," Gabriel said as he came to her, tightened the blanket around her cold body, held her close.

"You're sure?"

"I'm sure."

Lolly hadn't thought she'd ever be glad to hear that anyone was dead, but pure relief washed through her. She rested her head on Gabriel's shoulder, wallowing in the strength and warmth of it. "I killed her," she whispered.

Gabriel stepped back, made her look him in the eye. How could he be so calm? So steady? The flame on the stove flickered, casting strange shadows over his face. "Good job," he said briefly, paying a very subtle compliment to her strength by not sugarcoating anything.

Lolly squared her shoulders. "I'm not sorry," she said. "She was coming after you with a knife. She would've killed us both."

Lolly took the few steps that separated her from the stove and turned the knob that killed the flame, plunging the room into darkness. "I don't want soup, I don't want anything that comes out of this damned kitchen," she muttered.

"We need to eat," he argued.

"I have breakfast bars," she said, hugging the blanket to her cold body and walking away. If she never set foot in this kitchen again she'd be perfectly happy.

Gabriel followed her out of the kitchen, so when she stumbled on the end of the blanket—halfway through the dining room—he was there to catch her, to keep her from falling on her face. After everything that had happened, to trip over the trailing end of a blanket shouldn't be traumatic, but tears welled up in her eyes. Gabriel heard them, saw them, maybe felt them, and lifted her into his arms. She let him, without a word of protest that she was perfectly capable of taking care of herself. At the moment she didn't feel capable at all. He whispered soothing words. She didn't pay any attention to what those words were, but she felt the intent, the comfort, to the pit of her soul.

The living room was like another world: warm, lit by the fire, quiet. What was left of the storm raged on the other side of the window, beyond the sturdy walls, but for the first time tonight that storm was separate and unimportant. They were alive. They had survived a threat that was greater than the storm.

Gabriel lowered her to the sofa and sat beside her, continuing to hold her close. Lolly wanted to stop shaking, but couldn't. It wasn't the cold that made her tremble, not this time.

"I think I'll hire someone to come in and pack up everything that's left," she said, her gaze on the fire, her body fitting nicely against Gabriel's.

"Probably not a bad idea."

"If I thought we could make it safely to town tonight, I'd be out that door in five minutes. I can't come back here after this. I don't ever want to see this house again."

"Too bad." His voice was a rumbling whisper, as if he were simply thinking out loud.

Lolly lifted her head and looked at him. "What?" Surely she hadn't heard him correctly. "Seriously?" How could he think she could ever look at this house as home again? Why would anyone in their right mind want to return after a night like this one?

"Wilson Creek won't be the same without a Helton around, even if just part-time."

"Wilson Creek will survive," she argued.

Gabriel sighed. "I guess so, but how am I supposed to ask you out whenever I come back to visit if you're in Portland instead of here?"

She didn't know what shocked her most, that he'd

consider asking her out, or that he knew details of her current living situation. "How do you know I live in Portland?"

He shrugged broad shoulders. "I must've heard someone mention it. Mom, probably. Which reminds me, you're invited to stay at the house until the roads are clear."

"That's very nice," she said, knowing without a doubt that the invitation had been Valerie McQueen's idea.

She turned toward the fire, finding Gabriel's solemn face somehow disturbing, and her gaze fell on the drugs and needles sitting on the coffee table. She all but jumped from the couch, reaching for the plastic bags, intending to toss everything into the fire. Gabriel grabbed her hand before she could touch anything.

"Evidence," he said simply. "Leave everything right where it is."

She turned on him, irrationally angry. "I'm supposed to leave this crap sitting on my mother's coffee table all night?"

"Yes."

"That's ridiculous. It's . . . it's obscene! If Niki had died in the kitchen, would you have just left her there all night?"

"Yep. I'm a cop, honey—a military cop, but still a cop. You don't disturb a scene until the investigation is finished."

It was good to feel something besides fear, so she

fully embraced her annoyance. "So Niki and Darwin are both dead, and yet somehow they're still in charge."

Gabriel snorted, completely unflustered. "No, *I'm* in charge, and my dad will have my hide and yours if I fuck around with the evidence."

"So I have to sit here and look at *this* all night." She pointed to the coffee table, silently thanking her lucky stars that Niki had had the grace to die outside. If the body was in the kitchen, under her roof, she'd be trekking down the mountain tonight, ice or no ice.

Gabriel got to his feet. She expected him to take her in his arms again, but he didn't. He placed two steady hands on her shoulders and looked her directly in the eye. "I'm going upstairs to collect a sheet to cover the coffee table and a couple of blankets and pillows for us. You're going to pick out some dry clothes and get dressed. Then I'm going to heat up some soup . . ."

"I'm not going back in that kitchen . . ." Lolly said forcefully.

". . . and bring a couple of bowls in here," he continued without pausing, "so we can get something hot into our bellies. We'll save the breakfast bars for the trip down the mountain."

"How can you be so calm?" she asked, annoyed and grateful and mad at herself because a part of her was still scared.

"What choice do I have?" he responded.

Lolly felt a wave of release wash through her.

Naturally, he was right. If they both panicked they'd simply create yet another disaster, and God knows she'd had enough disaster for one night.

"I'll get dressed," she said in a more controlled voice. "You do what you have to do."

Gabriel leaned in then, and did what he'd neglected to do earlier. He kissed her. This wasn't a "let's get busy" kiss, it was a reassuring, warm, very pleasant connection that served to remind her that she was not alone, and at the same time very effectively took her mind off the night's horrors—for a few precious seconds.

She felt the kiss in her gut. Her earlier panic, which had fluttered inside her as if it were a physical thing trying to escape, faded.

She could do this. *They* could do this.

The kiss didn't last long enough, but it did the trick. She laid her hand on Gabriel's cheek, felt the rough stubble there. "All right," she said softly. "I'm okay now."

She turned to the fireplace and its welcome flame, listened as Gabriel rushed up the stairs.

Realistically, this adventure was far from over. The walk into town tomorrow would be dangerous and difficult. But it wasn't tomorrow yet, and tonight she was safe, warm, and sheltered.

She felt a bit Scarlett O'Hara-ish. She'd deal with tomorrow when it arrived.

Chapter Thirteen

Gabriel leaned his head back against the couch and closed his eyes. Chicken noodle soup out of a can had never tasted so good. The simple pleasure of not being out in the cold, of having a fire, of knowing he and Lolly were safe for the night—it was a fine feeling, one to be treasured even if just for a while.

The gas fireplace didn't crackle like a wood-burning stove, but he didn't have to worry about feeding it logs so that was a fair tradeoff. Lolly didn't know exactly how much propane was left in the tank, but she did tell him it hadn't been serviced for a while. She'd estimated that there would be enough for her stay, so they should be good for the night. A few hours more, that was all they needed.

"Tell me about your son." Lolly leaned against him,

as she had since finishing her soup. Her body was finally warm—and clothed. The shared body heat was kind of a cliché, he supposed, but it was nice. With a dead meth freak on the back porch and another in the woods, and an arduous walk ahead of them, *nice* was a good thing. He might as well enjoy it while he could.

"What do you want to know?"

"Does he look like you or like his mother? Is he into baseball or art or music? Is he loud or quiet?" Her head rested comfortably against his shoulder. "Is it hard for you, having him live so far away?" This last question was delivered with a hesitation in her voice, as if she wasn't certain it was a question that should be asked.

Gabriel never minded talking about Sam. There were times when he'd realized that he'd said too much, that he was boring whoever was listening—though they were usually too polite to say so. Since she'd asked, he was glad to answer. "Sam looks like me, but he has Mariane's eyes. He's not big for his age but he's not too small, either. He's into baseball, definitely, and basketball. Believe it or not, he's also a whiz at math. Well, a whiz for a seven-year-old. I'm not sure where he got that from, since math was not my best subject in school, and it drove Mariane nuts to have to balance the checkbook." It was strange to talk about his late wife without the usual rush of grief. Strange, but right. "He's definitely not quiet. Have you ever spent any significant time with a seven-year-old?"

"No," she said softly.

"Well, they're bundles of energy, and Sam is no exception. He's either going full speed ahead or he's asleep." He took a deep breath before continuing. "And having him live so far away is more than hard, it's torture." He found himself explaining how Mariane's parents had stepped up to help after her death, how his father-in-law had been transferred to Texas, and though he'd tried to find another job, one that would keep him and his wife near to their grandson, in the end he'd had no choice but to move. It was that or be unemployed. Gabriel told Lolly how he'd tried to make the single dad thing work, something he'd never really talked about before in any but the simplest way, not even with his own parents.

"Babysitters, neighbors, Mariane's friends, my friends' wives . . . everyone did what they could to help, but in the end my schedule was so erratic it became a problem. Sam had no continuity. He never knew where he'd be, who would keep him when I was working night shift or was called away suddenly. Here he has stability. He knows where he's going to sleep at night."

"It's a high price to pay," Lolly said. "For both of you."

He'd been telling himself the situation was temporary, that he'd find a nanny he could afford so his son could be home at night, but with every week that passed there was a growing fear that he'd never be able to make the proper arrangements. He was a sergeant in the army, and though he made a decent living, he didn't make enough to pay someone twenty grand a year, which was the bare minimum for full-time child care.

He didn't want his son to grow up with an absent father who visited when he could, but in his darkest moments he didn't see how he could avoid that, at least right now. Sam's grandparents would effectively become his parents, and his father would be an afterthought, an occasional visitor who disrupted the everyday routine. Lolly was right; the sacrifice was a high price to pay for stability.

"We'll make it work," he said. "Whatever's best for Sam, that's what I'll do." He was anxious to change the subject. "What about you? Married, engaged, divorced . . ."

"None of the above. I do date, on occasion, but there hasn't been anything serious in a long while."

"Why not?" She was pretty, smart, and if what had happened in the shower was any indication, a wildcat in the sack. She had taken him by surprise, but then just about everything she'd done since he'd climbed that rickety ladder a few hours ago had surprised him. Whoever would have thought that he'd come to admire Lolly Helton? She had been out of her element from the get-go, but she had toughed it out, and even come to his aid during both of his battles with Darwin and Niki. Her inner strength, especially concerning

Niki, brought up a deep sense of respect. That couldn't have been easy for her, but she'd done what had to be done, and she hadn't collapsed afterward.

He wasn't about to admit that he'd expected less of her though, because the one thing he didn't want to do was hurt her feelings or get on her bad side. To his astonishment, he liked her too damn much, liked everything he'd learned about her tonight.

"Maybe I'm too picky." Her answer brought his attention back to the question he'd asked. She sighed. "Maybe I'm unlucky. I don't know. The simple answer is, it's just never happened for me. Love, that is," she said more softly. "I have certain expectations and I don't want to settle for just any halfway decent man because thirty crept up on me and desperation set in."

He couldn't see the Lolly he used to know or the woman he'd come to know tonight being desperate to land a man. She'd survived a tough situation without falling apart, and while she leaned on him—literally and figuratively—she was far from being fragile and needy.

And he'd forever remember the image of her rushing after Niki, coming to his defense even though she was scared half out of her wits—and naked, to boot.

"What about you?" she asked, as if an idea had just occurred to her. "Has there been anyone since your wife died?" He could hear the hint of discomfort in her voice, as she wondered if she'd had sex with a man who was committed to another.

"No."

He was certain Lolly didn't expect that her relief would be so evident to him, but her sigh and the way her body relaxed told it all. So, she was pretty, smart, not desperate, and she had morals. Otherwise the thought that she might've had impulsive sex with a man who was involved with another woman wouldn't have bothered her at all.

"Did you mean what you said earlier?" she asked. "About asking me out if you came home on leave and I was around."

"I wouldn't have said it if I didn't. Why? Would you say yes?"

"Maybe. But only if you promised that our second date would be less exciting than the first."

He laughed, surprising her and himself. This wasn't a night for laughter—or hadn't been until now. "This is a date?"

"You saw me naked and you fed me dinner." There was a touch of humor in her voice. "Sounds like a bang-up date to me."

Gabriel had wondered a time or two what his first date after Mariane's death would be like, if he ever found the right woman—and the courage to move forward. He'd sure as hell never pictured anything like this, never by any stretch of the imagination thought it might be Lolly Helton, of all people, who for the first time in three years made him feel both physical and emotional attraction. He wanted to have sex with her again, he wanted to share mundane things with her, he wanted to find out what made her laugh, what made her cry, what colors she liked, her favorite flower. Lolly made him feel as if there might be a real life out there again, a life both full and ordinary. He'd had that with Mariane, and her sudden death had left him so empty that only having Sam had given him the strength to go on.

He and Lolly had been through a very stressful few hours that made their sense of intimacy, their connection, far more intense than if they'd met again under normal circumstances. But would they have given each other a chance if the circumstances had been normal? Had it taken a crisis to make them see each other as they were now, rather than how they'd been fifteen years ago?

But the connection was definitely there, and all of a sudden he felt the promise of his future rather than the loss of his past. They'd have to go slow, he figured, give themselves as well as Sam time to adjust to everything, give themselves time to see if things really would work out between them, instead of rushing in and maybe making a mistake that would upset Sam's world even more.

But they had time. He smiled, thinking about how much fun they'd have.

Lolly did her best to forget what had happened today, and she pushed her worry about tomorrow out of her head. The howling wind had stopped and icy rain no longer pelted the windows. But the roads would still be coated with ice, and she still heard the occasional crack and crash of a falling tree or heavy limb. There was no telling what she and Gabriel would encounter after they walked out her door tomorrow, headed for Wilson Creek and safety.

At the moment she was happy to be right here, warm and in Gabriel's loose but secure embrace.

As a teenager she'd had such a crush on him, and she'd been supremely annoyed with him for not returning, or even being aware of, her tender feelings. Looking back, she realized that there had been absolutely no reason for him to know what she'd been feeling. She hadn't told him, or anyone else. She hadn't even looked his way, unless he picked a fight with her and she responded. At fifteen, she hadn't been so logical. Though to be honest, what fifteen-year-old was well acquainted with logic?

There was something very appealing about a man who talked with such evident love about his son, who sacrificed everything so that his child could have a secure and happy home. She worried less about tomorrow's long walk to town than she would have otherwise, because she knew Gabriel would not only do everything in his power to get them there as soon as possible, he'd also be damn sure to get them there safely—if not for her, or for himself, then for Sam.

Sleep was creeping up on her fast. She could feel oblivion, welcome, certain. But she wasn't ready to fall just yet.

"I'll probably be back in Wilson Creek a time or two in the next few months," she said softly. "Even if I hire someone to pack up the house, there will be papers to sign to put it on the market, and then when it sells I'll have to come here to see to the legalities." She was almost positive she could handle the details long distance, but . . . maybe she didn't want to.

"I try to get back at least every other month," Gabriel said casually. "Sometimes it's just for a couple of days, but I have to see Sam whenever I get the chance."

Duh. All his talk of a date was just a way to kill time, maybe an attempt to make her forget what had happened tonight. When Gabriel came back to Wilson Creek he wanted to be with his family, most particularly his son, not a girl he barely remembered from high school.

And then he added, "You should meet Sam. When it warms up we can go fishing." She didn't immediately respond, so he added, "You don't fish, do you?"

"I'm world-class at reaching into the freezer and pulling out some filets," she said, smiling. "I could probably learn. From what I've seen it doesn't appear to be too demanding." She tried to picture a warm summer day, the lake, the three of them fishing and maybe picnicking on a large, checkered blanket . . . and she couldn't do it. The picture she tried to create in her mind didn't quite come together.

She didn't belong. Lolly realized she wasn't a part

of the picture and never would be. Still, it was a nice illusion, a pleasant way to push aside reality for a while. "I make great chocolate chip cookies and a killer pasta salad. We could have a picnic, too." She closed her eyes, and for a moment she was there, she belonged in that picture. Maybe it wasn't real, maybe it would never be real, but as she drifted toward sleep she got caught up in the fantasy, then sleep overtook her and she went under fast and deep.

The sunlight sparkled like diamonds on the ice-coated trees; overhead, the sky was a pure, crisp blue. It would be a breathtaking scene, Lolly thought, if she was looking at it through a window with a blazing fire behind her, or maybe standing on a beach in Florida looking at a postcard. Instead she was part of the picture, which included cold air, a slick surface beneath her feet, and the occasional obstacle of a fallen limb or tree, for good measure—in case walking downhill on a sheet of ice wasn't challenge enough.

Not knowing when she'd be able to make it back, Lolly had stuffed what she needed in her pockets. Keys, driver's license, cash, credit cards, cell phone, which would be useless until they reached the highway. Everything else had been left behind. There was no telling when she'd be able to collect her Mercedes. She might have to arrange alternate transportation to Portland and come back for her vehicle once the roads were clear. That all depended on how bad things were in town, and how badly blocked the roads up the mountain were.

At least her clothing today was better suited to the weather. She had on her own thick, hooded coat, her boots, her gloves. At least the sun was shining, and they could see where they were going. At least they weren't being chased by homicidal drug addicts. All in all, today was much better than last night, even though the air was so cold she could barely breathe it and had to keep her nose and mouth covered with a scarf. The sunlight on the ice was almost blinding, and both she and Gabriel wore shades. Compared to last night, though, this was a walk in the park. It was cold, sure, but there was no cutting wind, no rain. All that was left were the remnants of the storm—the fallen trees, the icy ground, the crisp, cold air.

The weight of the ice was still a burden for the trees, and that would be their greatest obstacle as they made their way down the mountain. Not long after leaving the house they heard the now-familiar crack, followed by a crash. Gabriel's head had snapped around at the sound and he'd stopped, listening hard as if he might be able to tell where that tree was, how close it might be. The fall was in the distance, in the woods that surrounded Lolly's childhood home, but it was telling—a warning, of sorts. They couldn't get off the mountain without walking beneath trees. None of the ice was melting, the air was still too cold, so any of the trees could go at any time. They would have to be on constant guard against the weighted, weakened limbs overhead.

This wasn't over, not by a long shot.

Gabriel stayed close, either right beside her or directly ahead of her, depending on the width of the grassy strip and the thickness of the vegetation, as they walked along the side of the driveway. Though he hadn't said much, he had to be as worried about the treefall as she was. That was why he often glanced overhead and, when possible, followed a path that didn't take them directly beneath the overhanging limbs.

They were halfway down the driveway when they came to a splintered, icy tree that had fallen crookedly across their path. Gabriel straddled the tree, offered Lolly a hand, and helped her up and over. Walking on an icy surface was tough enough, but maneuvering over obstacles only made things harder. If they'd had enough food and propane they would've been better off staying at the house until help arrived . . . at least in her opinion. Gabriel might've had other ideas, since he'd left his son behind to rescue her and was anxious to get home.

Hiking wasn't her thing. She wasn't into athletics at all, other than admiring the great physical condition of professional athletes; she was definitely a woman who admired a great tight end when she saw one. Her layers of clothing made her feel awkward and unwieldy, while Gabriel managed to remain his usual capable, annoyingly perfect self. He'd always been athletic, and, yes, he had a great tight end. If he hadn't been wearing his own heavy coat, she'd at least have been able to admire his personal scenery. Thank goodness he didn't know she was imagining his butt; he continued on, steadfast and skillful, leading the way with aplomb.

She didn't do anything with aplomb, even when she wasn't hampered by layer upon layer of clothing. At least if she fell she'd be well cushioned when she hit the ground.

Gabriel looked great. Good-looking, muscled . . . really great eyes, a blue-green hazel ringed by inky lashes. He was bigger than he'd been in high school, definitely older, but those eyes hadn't changed at all. Lolly had to forcibly stop herself from getting carried away. She tried to call upon reason, to think clearly. He'd saved her life, so there was probably some instinctive attraction going on that had absolutely nothing to do with who he was. Add the fact that they'd been skin to skin, that he'd been inside her, and she shouldn't expect anything less than total infatuation.

Oh, who was she kidding? She'd always had the hots for him—not to the point that she'd spent the last fifteen years pining over him, but enough so that when she saw him again that old interest immediately flared to life again.

When she was safely over the log that blocked her driveway, Gabriel held on to her for a moment longer than was necessary, making sure her footing was solid—not that she was in any hurry to move away.

"I have soup and coffee in the truck," he said. "We'll take a short break there, and if a tree hasn't fallen on it, we can get in the truck and get warm."

After the hours the truck had been sitting, she had no hope at all that either soup or coffee would be warm, but it was food and she'd take it. The breakfast bars weren't going to last nearly long enough. "Good idea." It was a long way to Wilson Creek, and the trip was best faced in small chunks. To the end of the driveway. To the curve where the old Morrison house used to be. To the hill where there was a break in the tree line, where the sun would surely shine. To the highway . . . and from there they'd start all over again, as they walked to the McQueen house.

Where she'd be a literal fifth wheel.

After taking several steps without any problem, without warning, Lolly's right foot flew out from under her. She instinctively flailed for a low lying limb, but as she grabbed it the thin, frozen twig snapped. Gabriel grabbed her, making sure she didn't land on her ass. He held her close, secure, and she took a moment to wallow in his body heat and solid build. Gabriel McQueen was like a rock. Without him, where would she be right now? She couldn't let her mind go there.

Lolly's heart pounded as she tried to catch her breath. She knew what a disaster a bad fall would be. She was already sore, bruised, and shaken. All she needed was to break a bone or sprain an ankle. If she thought she was a burden to Gabriel now . . .

"You okay?" he asked.

When she nodded her head he released her, and she moved forward.

One step at a time.

Gabriel had known the trek down the mountain would be a tough one, hour upon hour of watching every step and being alert to the dangers all around.

After stopping at the truck to get warm—no trees having fallen on the truck—to drink some lukewarm coffee and soup, and to retrieve his weatherproof hat, he and Lolly resumed their trek. Lolly didn't grumble, hadn't uttered a word of complaint, but she'd already started breathing harder and favoring her bruised right side.

He took her hand as they met a hill, knowing that on the other side of that rise was a sharp dip in the earth that would not be easy to take. They leaned into the climb, watching each step, breathing hard, not wasting precious energy by speaking.

Gabriel kept telling himself it could be worse. As far as mountains in this part of the country went, this was a small one, not high enough for good skiing. Some might even call it a big hill, instead of a mountain. Walking down was doable, and they should be thankful for that. The storm had stopped. If they'd had to walk out in the wind and falling rain, the walk would take twice as long and be ten times as dangerous. If either he or Lolly had been hurt last night, shot or slashed with a knife, then they'd be separated, the mobile one hiking alone to town for help, the other left behind. And if they'd both been hurt . . .

Would his dad figure that he'd been stranded by the storm and that all was well, or would he be worried and doing what he could to get up this road? Lolly had said that when Darwin and Niki broke in, she was on her way out to stay with the Richards. Would Mrs. Richard be worried enough to call the sheriff's office and report that Lolly hadn't arrived? Or would she just assume that Lolly had wasted time and let the storm catch her on the mountain? Lots of possibilities, and he had no way of knowing what to expect. He might as well proceed as if he and Lolly were entirely on their own. For now, they were.

Halfway up the hill a patch of sun warmed the ground. That heat and light was a welcome relief— though he knew it wouldn't last. Where the sunshine touched the ground, the going was easier. They could even take a few steps on the roadway, when the shoulder was narrow and too close to a drop-off for comfort. He didn't bother to drop Lolly's hand, even when the walking was less slippery for a few precious steps.

"Not so bad, huh?" he asked.

Lolly was breathless when she answered, "Speak for yourself, McQueen."

He would've turned to give her an encouraging smile, to tell her that they were making great time, but then he reached the top of the hill and got a good look at what lay ahead.

There weren't just one or two fallen trees across the road, there was one right after another for as far as he could see. Some lay there alone, with stretches of blessedly untouched roadway on either side. Others crisscrossed, one trunk and another . . . and another . . . blocking their way. Some they could go over, as they'd gone over the one on the driveway. Others were too big, or the limbs were too tangled. They were going to have to go around some of the blockage, detouring into the woods, wasting precious minutes.

"Fuck," he muttered.

"Right now?" Lolly joked, but out of the corner of his eye he saw her straighten her spine and lift her chin. She looked a little ridiculous, the way she was bundled up, but she also looked strong. And kind of amazing. She pulled in a deep breath.

"I am *not* going to get away from Niki and Darwin and survive a cat-and-mouse chase through the icy rain and in my own kitchen just to give up now," she said. Her eyes narrowed. "I'll be damned if I'm going to sit down and cry, even if that's the first impulse that comes to mind." She looked at him, and he saw the shine of tears in her eyes. "It's going to be a long day. Distract me." She moved to the side of the road and started her descent. "You must have hundreds of cute and funny stories about Sam. Tell me a few. Make me laugh."

Gabriel didn't feel much like laughing at the moment, but thinking about Sam waiting for his dad to come home drove him forward.

Chapter Fourteen

There were moments when Lolly didn't think she could take another step. Her feet hurt. Everything hurt. For a while Gabriel and his stories kept her moving, but now it was the sound of chain saws that kept her motivated. It was impossible to tell exactly where the sounds were coming from. Crews might be working in town, and the noise just carried. Then again, maybe the workers were on this very road. Maybe just over the next hill . . . or the next.

"When I buy a house in Portland, it's going to be on completely flat land. With close neighbors. And constant five-bar cell service."

Gabriel looked over his shoulder. "You're planning on buying a house?"

"I've been thinking about it," she said. "I have a

nice apartment, but rent is just money down the drain. They keep saying it's a good time to buy."

He made a sound, like a soft grunt from deep in his throat. "I didn't know you planned to put down roots in Portland."

"I have a good job there. Friends. I'm . . . comfortable."

Again he made that grunting noise.

At the moment *comfortable* seemed like a decidedly good thing to Lolly. She liked comfortable. She enjoyed a life where there were no surprises.

And then she got a surprise.

"Before you buy a house, you should come visit me in North Carolina. Maybe you'd like it better there."

The comment left her dumbfounded, but she didn't have time to read too much into the invitation, because Gabriel crested the hill they were climbing, and stopped. She was directly behind him, so close she almost crashed into his back. Instead she moved to stand beside him. There, in the distance—but blessedly not *too* far away—sat a massive truck with a crane built into the bed. A four-man crew was cutting limbs and tree trunks and moving them off the roadway with the crane. They'd already cut a swath from the highway.

Lolly was so relieved, her knees almost buckled out from under her. She leaned into Gabriel in sheer relief. He took her hand and squeezed. "Almost there, Lollipop."

She wanted to ask Gabriel more about his impromptu invitation, but the time for that question had come and gone in an instant, and she'd missed it.

Knowing that help was so close spurred them both forward. Gabriel continued to hold her hand. Whether to make sure she kept up or to maintain a connection she didn't know . . . and was afraid to ask. Every insecurity, the shyness she'd thought she'd defeated years ago, came rushing to the surface. Gabriel might ask her to visit him, when there was no one in the world but the two of them and the rush of survival was still warm within them. But now . . . what would happen now, with the real world intruding?

It seemed to take forever to reach the road crew, who spotted Gabriel and Lolly from a distance and waved enthusiastically. As they came nearer the one in the front—Justin Temple, who hadn't changed much since Lolly had moved away from Wilson Creek—called out in a booming, deep voice. "The sheriff said we might run into you two, but I didn't expect to see you so soon. We've got coffee and sandwiches," he added, and then he unclipped a radio from his belt and spoke to someone on the other end of the line.

This road should've been low priority, but thanks to the sheriff it hadn't been. Lolly knew there were other crews out there, clearing roads in town and in the neighborhoods just beyond, and she could only be grateful that she'd gotten herself stranded with the sheriff's son—and that Harlan McQueen carried a lot of weight around here.

The coffee was fairly fresh, fairly hot, and tasted

better than any coffee she'd ever had. She was so exhausted she could only manage a few bites of the sandwich, but she ate what she could, then she and Gabriel sat on the back of the truck and waited for the sheriff, who Justin said was already on his way. Now that she wasn't moving the cold felt sharper, but at the same time it felt good to just *sit*. Gabriel put his arm around her, hugged her to him.

The crew continued to work, though she suspected that since she and Gabriel had shown up, they might soon be sent to another, more heavily populated area. She still couldn't count on getting to her car anytime soon.

"I guess I could catch a bus back to Portland," she said. She wasn't sure when they'd be running again, but maybe it would be no more than a couple of days.

"What's the rush?" Gabriel asked casually.

"I can't do a thing with the house until the roads are cleared, I can't even get to my car. If it's like this all over town that could take days . . . even weeks. I can't stay here for weeks."

"Why not?"

Lolly opened her mouth to answer, but said nothing. She'd been invited to a friend's house for Christmas Eve, but on Christmas Day she'd be alone. The office wouldn't open until after New Year's, so she'd have that week to take care of a few chores around the house. She'd planned to clean her closets and go through the pantry getting rid of all the expired food she'd never used. Maybe watch some movies, organize her DVDs and CDs, try some new recipes. In other words, nothing of any importance.

Gabriel touched her cheek and gently forced her to look him in the eye. Without a word, he kissed her, the touch light and easy, familiar, as if they'd kissed a thousand times. When he pulled his mouth away he said, "Stay with us. I'd like you to get to know Sam. Mom would love to have you, and so would I."

"You've already had me." The words were out of her mouth before she could stop them.

Gabriel smiled. "So I have, and I've been thinking about a repeat. What about you?"

There was no ignoring what had happened in the shower, but at the same time she felt kind of clueless. Yes, she'd been icy cold, frightened, desperate . . . but she wouldn't have wanted just anyone the way she'd wanted Gabriel. She wasn't made that way.

"So, what is this, exactly?" she asked.

Her timing continued to be terrible. At that moment they heard the roar of an engine and the loud jangle of chains on tires making their way down the icy road. Gabriel grinned when he saw the sheriff's four-wheel drive, with his dad behind the wheel. He jumped off the truck and turned to slide his hands under Lolly's coat and grip her waist, then he lifted her down. Lolly smiled, too, but that smile was forced.

Because she knew from here on out she and Gabriel wouldn't be alone again. The adventure was over; she'd been rescued too soon.

———————

Gabriel barely waited for the SUV to come to a stop at his parents' house before he opened the door and stepped carefully onto the salted driveway, new energy in his step in spite of his exhaustion. He and Lolly had to give official statements, but not even that was going to keep him from seeing Sam first. His dad had told him how worried Sam had been when Gabriel hadn't come home as promised last night. The storm had done nothing to ease the kid's fears.

When he reached the door, he met his mother— who was physically restraining Sam. She had him by the collar, the same way she'd corralled Gabriel a time or two. Valerie said, "See, I told you he was all right," and let Sam go.

"Dad!" Once he was free, Sam burst forward and up, into Gabriel's arms. Gabriel held on tight, and so did Sam.

"I thought you weren't coming back," Sam said, his head buried in Gabriel's shoulder. He began sobbing. "I thought you had a wreck, or got frozen, or a tree fell on your truck. Gran said you were fine, she said you knew how to take care of yourself, but I dreamed you weren't ever coming back."

Gabriel's heart constricted. A child shouldn't have such fears, but loss wasn't new to Sam. He patted Sam's narrow back, instinctively rocking his child from side to side in the universal comforting motion.

"It wasn't that bad. I just got stuck at Lolly's house because the roads froze sooner than I expected."

Sam lifted his head and looked directly at Gabriel. His tear-wet eyes narrowed. "Lolly. That's the stupidest name I ever heard."

"It's short for Lorelei."

Gabriel half turned to see that Lolly and his dad had entered the kitchen behind him. He'd been so caught up in his reunion with Sam, he hadn't heard them come in. Lolly, who had offered the explanation for her name, smiled gently, showing no outward sign of the trauma she'd experienced. For Sam's sake, he knew, and for that he was grateful.

Sam was not appeased. He'd been terrified, and obviously Lolly was to blame. "If my name was Lorelei I'd make people call me something else, too. That's even stupider than *Lolly.*"

"Sam," Gabriel chided gently. "That's rude. Apologize."

He ducked his head, his small jaw set. "Sorry," he mumbled, spitting out the word without an ounce of real regret. He wouldn't overtly disobey, but that was about as far as he was willing to go.

Lolly took no offense—or at least, she didn't appear to. She took a step forward, moving closer. "I imagine you're pretty mad at me for dragging your dad out of the house in a storm."

A sullen Sam nodded. "You shoulda left before the storm got here."

"I understand that," Lolly said. "Ah . . . something happened, and I couldn't leave." She reached out to tuck a wayward strand of hair away from Sam's face. "And I'm sure you understand that your daddy is a real, live, honest-to-goodness hero, in a world that needs all the heroes it can get."

"Well, *yeah*," Sam agreed. "Duh."

Gabriel watched Lolly bite back a laugh. She was doing this right, not coming on too strong, not trying to act like Sam's best friend when they'd just met. "You look very much like him. Are you a hero, too?"

At that, Sam's spine straightened. With Gabriel holding him, he was able to look Lolly in the eye for a moment, before he nodded.

"I'm so glad to hear that," Lolly said with a friendly smile. "The world needs heroes like you and your dad."

Sam looked closely at Lolly's bruised face. "What happened to you?" He pointed to her cheek, and Gabriel held his breath. He couldn't protect Sam from all the ugliness in the world, but the kid didn't need to know that it had all but landed on his doorstep.

Lolly gently placed a hand over her cheek. "I fell," she said simply. "That was before your dad arrived, and I have to tell you, he saved me from falling several times."

"The ice is slippery," Sam said in an almost grown-up voice. "Gran wouldn't let me go outside, even to meet Dad."

"Your Gran is a very smart woman," Lolly said sincerely.

Gabriel could see the wheels in his son's head turning, as he sized up the situation and the woman before him. "Sorry I made fun of your name," he said, more sincerely this time.

"You're not the first," she said in a confidential tone, as if there weren't three other adults listening in. "Your father used to call me . . ." She glanced around, then leaned in and whispered in Sam's ear. "Lollipop."

Sam started to giggle, and Gabriel put the kid on his feet. He didn't go far, though. Sam stayed close, leaning into Gabriel, occasionally grabbing on to his clothing, or his hand, to make sure he didn't go away again.

Valerie McQueen, always prepared, had a spread ready for them. Soup, sandwiches, coffee, cookies. Gabriel and Lolly sat at the kitchen table, Sam perched on Gabriel's knee, and ate until they couldn't get another bite down. It didn't take Sam long to relax with Lolly, or to release the remnants of his fear that his dad wasn't coming home. "Relaxed" didn't mean exactly friendly, but even as an infant Sam had always taken a while to warm up to strange adults.

For someone who didn't have kids, Lolly was good with Sam. Before he'd moved Sam to Maine, the friends—his and Mariane's—who'd spent time with Sam tended to smother him with sympathy. That sympathy was deserved, but after a while it didn't do the kid any good. Lolly talked to Sam almost like he was an adult, and the kid responded.

When she started telling Sam stories about his dad as a child, though, Gabriel had to interfere. He didn't want his kid—or his parents—hearing how he'd tormented Lolly. He called time-out and Lolly laughed— a real, honest laugh that warmed him to his bones.

Sam only called her Lollipop once, and they both immediately fell into a fit of laughter while Gabriel and his folks looked on, bemused and surprised. And Gabriel realized that at some point in the last twenty-four hours, his world had shifted.

Lolly leaned her head back and closed her eyes, letting the hot water do its work on her tired, over-worked, once-frozen muscles. Usually she jumped in the shower, got clean, and got out. It had been a long while since she'd indulged in a real, soaking bath.

The McQueen bathroom was larger than the one at the old house, built years later when so much space was no longer a luxury but a necessity. The bathtub was wide and deep; the counter on the other side of the square room was long and crowded with soaps, towels, shampoos, and two flickering candles. This house still had electricity, though much of Wilson Creek did not. Lolly wasn't taking any chances, though, hence the candles. If there was a disruption in the power, she wasn't going to be plunged into darkness—not tonight.

After Sam had gone to bed, she and Gabriel had

given their statements to Sheriff McQueen. Gabriel's dad was glad that they were both safe, and at the same time incensed that meth addicts had invaded his county. As soon as it was practicable, road and power crews would make their way up the mountain to the house. And still it would be days, maybe weeks, before they reached what was left of Darwin and Niki.

Which meant Lolly was going to be without her car for a while. That was the least of her worries . . .

She was roused out of a near sleep by a soft knock, following by the rattling of the doorknob, which she'd locked behind her.

"I'll be right out," she called, gathering the strength to rise from the still-warm water.

"Don't move," a familiar deep voice called. The doorknob rattled again, the lock set in the knob popped, and the door swung open. Lolly grabbed a wet washcloth and positioned it across her chest in a poor, last second attempt at modesty.

Gabriel slid into the room and closed—and locked—the door behind him.

"You've just proven to me that the lock on that door is useless," she said. Maybe she should be more shocked, more shy. But she wasn't.

He held aloft a bent paper clip. "I grew up in this house. All the interior locks do is warn someone who tries to get in that the room is occupied."

"And yet you didn't take the hint."

He smiled down at her, and she wished she had a couple more washcloths handy. "Want me to leave?"

She knew if she said yes, he'd go. "No."

Gabriel turned off the harsh overhead light, plunging the room into near darkness. The candles provided flickering light. He unbuttoned his shirt and slid it off, then unfastened and unzipped his jeans and stepped out of them. Socks and underwear followed. Heaven above, he was gorgeous and tempting.

"Your folks . . ."

"Are asleep," he said as he stepped into the water. "Dead to the world, just like Sam. I don't think any of them got much sleep last night."

"Neither did you," Lolly said as she scooted back, making a place for Gabriel to sit, facing her. He sat down slowly, and the level of water in the tub rose almost to the edge. The slightest movement would send water sloshing onto the floor. "Why aren't you asleep?"

"Same reason you're here instead of tucked into a warm bed, I imagine."

Her mind wouldn't stop spinning. She didn't know what tomorrow would bring. Her world had been turned upside down. Of course she couldn't sleep!

Gabriel looked her in the eye. They were naked, wet, face-to-face. She wanted nothing more than to reach out and hold him, but she didn't make that move. "Why are you here?" Maybe it should have been obvious, but she was asking more than about just the sex.

He reached out and touched her bruised cheek

with strong and surprisingly gentle hands. "I have a favor to ask."

"You did save my life," she said, wondering what kind of favor it might be. Since they were both naked, she had a clue . . .

"Don't go back to Portland just yet."

Even though he'd mentioned that this afternoon, as they'd made their way down the mountain, it wasn't exactly what she'd been expecting. Reality had descended with a bang, and even though she loved this house, this home, this family . . . she didn't belong here. "Why not?"

"Stay here, spend Christmas with us." Gabriel stopped and took a deep breath. "Let's see where this goes."

Her insides leapt and danced.

"Let's see where *we* go," he clarified, though no clarification was necessary.

"I can do that," she whispered.

He leaned toward her, peeled the washcloth from her breasts and tossed it aside, kissed her, and sent a bit of water over the lip of the tub. She barely noticed.

"And stop talking about buying a house in Portland. At least until you've visited North Carolina a time or two. It's much warmer there."

"And you're there."

He made an affirmative humming sound as he continued to move forward.

Lolly felt all her cares, all her worries, unwinding,

fading away. "That doesn't seem at all like too much to ask, all things considered."

He put his mouth on hers again, and the kiss quickly took on a rhythm. Lolly wallowed in Gabriel's heat and hardness, she welcomed the kiss, the connection, the warmth they generated . . . a warmth that transformed her from the inside out.

Gabriel took his mouth from hers, but he didn't move far. His nose touched hers; he was a breath away. "Lollipop, can I lick you?"

"Yes," she said, wrapping her arms around Gabriel's neck and surging into him to send more water onto the floor. "Yes, you can."